"She's the chosen one, is she, Callum?"

Callum stopped in his tracks. "Who's choice?"

"Your family's, obviously. Yours, maybe." Morag's lips curved as she went on mischievously. "If her father's firm is building your hotel, you could get very good terms."

Callum laughed and shook his head. "What a mercenary you are. Rosalie's nice, but don't you think she's too young for me?"

Callum wouldn't change that much, Morag thought. He was experienced, brilliant and tough. Nor would Rosalie change. She would always be enchanting and no match for Callum.

"She'll get older," she said with only the faintest note of mockery. "I hope you'll be very happy."

"I hope so, too," he said, and the smile died on Morag's lips because Callum was not smiling. They were no longer talking of Rosalie....

Books by Jane Donnelly

HARLEQUIN ROMANCE

These books may be available at your local bookseller.

Don't miss any of our special offers. Write to us at the following address for information on our newest releases.

Harlequin Reader Service
P.O. Box 52040, Phoenix, AZ 85072-2040
Canadian address: P.O. Box 2800, Postal Station A,
5170 Yonge St., Willowdale, Ont.   M2N 6J3

To Cage a Whirlwind

Jane Donnelly

Harlequin Books

TORONTO • NEW YORK • LONDON
AMSTERDAM • PARIS • SYDNEY • HAMBURG
STOCKHOLM • ATHENS • TOKYO • MILAN

Original hardcover edition published in 1985
by Mills & Boon Limited

ISBN 0-373-02738-9

Harlequin Romance first edition January 1986

CHAPTER ONE

SHE saw her brother at the other end of the gallery and made her way towards him, slowly because he was occupied. This was an antiques market, in an old Tudor house in the Cotswolds; different dealers, in their sections, offering everything from jewellery to furniture. Alistair was at the antiquarian book department, talking to someone who might be a customer.

Morag Macdonald stopped half way down the gallery to look at him fondly. He was very handsome was her brother, with his coppery hair and his regular features. Wearing dark slacks and dark polo-necked sweater he looked responsible she thought, without being stuffy. He was the manager here and she felt that the customer should be taking his advice because her brother Alistair was a man you could trust.

Alistair wrote something down, a book to look out for probably, and the other man walked away; and a girl who was surrounded by clothes that had last seen the light of day in the thirties said, 'Why, hello Morag.'

Alistair had been in charge here for nearly two years but Morag's visits had been fleeting, she usually met him when he came up to London, but she was a girl who was remembered. Nearly as tall as her brother, her hair was a flaming red, and her eyes were green to his hazel. They had the same features, the high cheekbones and the wide mobile mouth. They were both stunners, and she was very proud of him.

Morag said hello to the girl and asked how she was keeping, and then Alistair spotted her and came rushing up. They hugged each other in mutual delight.

'Why didn't you ring?' he asked. 'What are you doing here?'

'The bad penny's turned up.' She smiled and so did he. 'I tried to 'phone you last night and got no answer, so,' she shrugged, 'I just came along.'

'Just like that?' She was carrying an overnight case. 'Just to see me?'

Sometimes she did modelling jobs and promotions work, but that hadn't brought her here today. 'Just to see you,' she said.

'You're staying the night?'

'Please. If that's all right.'

His apartment, on the top floor, had a spare bedroom and he had always stressed that it was there if she needed it. 'Now he said, 'Of course it's all right, come on up.'

He went ahead of her, up the oak staircase that was black with the patina of centuries, into the living room of his apartment. It looked good, like an extension of the antique furniture displays on this top floor, except that there was a 'phone, and cushions on the chairs, and a music centre along one wall.

'Drink?' he said.

'I'd like a coffee.' But he was opening a veneered corner cupboard, taking out a bottle and she said, 'It's a bit early in the day for me.' A kitchenette led off and she filled and switched on the kettle and watched through the door as her brother poured out a generous measure of whisky.

'I hope I haven't driven you to that.' She was joking but she hadn't seen this happen before, and he gulped half of it before he set the glass down. They had always kept in touch, 'phoning each other every few weeks if they didn't meet. They had been close all their lives. He was five years older than she and he had always been the big brother to whom she had turned at every small crisis.

is. He had problems that the individual stallholder did not have to face. She had enjoyed her afternoon, the hours passed quickly, and she was surprised when the building began to empty and the dealers began to pack up.

'See you tomorrow,' they said.

She answered, 'I'll be here,' and then Alistair came out of the office. Perhaps it was a holiday he needed, so far as she knew he hadn't taken a break this summer, because he did look tired although he was smiling when he reached her.

'Would you like to go up?' he said. 'I've got to lock up.'

This apartment, under the high beams of the roof, was going to be her home for a while. The living room she had left behind had been brightly and cheaply furnished, everything modern and mass produced, but there was an entirely different atmosphere in this room. There wasn't much in here that was less than a hundred years old, and she stood admiring the Queen Anne dresser, the Oriental rugs in rich blues and reds on the dark polished floor. Of all the rooms she had called home in the past nine years she felt she could grow fondest of this.

But she had better not gett too fond because she was not likely to be here for too long, and she went into the spare room and opened her weekend case. She hung a dress and a shirt in a cupboard, put slacks, a skirt, a couple of sweaters and undies in a little bow-fronted chest of drawers, and then washed her hands in the bathroom. Alistair could have plans for this evening but she had one. She would be staying in, getting an early night. It had been a long day and the strain of yesterday was still telling on her. She had had a sandwich during the afternoon, brought in from a pub, but that was all she had eaten since a slice of toast with her flatmates early this morning.

There had been no major crises in her life since she and their mother left the wild and beautiful Scottish island of Calla when Morag was thirteen, and came to live in a small guest house just along the coast from Bournemouth. Alistair had left the islands as soon as he left school. He was a born salesman and he adapted easily to city life. Alistair Macdonald had prospered and he had looked after Morag, after their mother died when Morag was sixteen.

She had been no handicap to him. She was bright as well as beautiful, and had earned a living, enjoying herself in a variety of jobs, and Alistair had always been there when she needed someone to talk to, or when she was undecided what to do. She had a restless streak that had kept her on the move, but she had always known that her brother was as near as the nearest telephone.

She hadn't seen him since Easter, it was October now. During the summer she had shared a flat with two other girls in Twickenham and worked in a flower shop. Now the shop had been sold to a family who intended staffing it themselves, and Morag was on the lookout for something else. Alistair knew this, she had discussed it with him, and he said, 'All completed is it, the takeover?'

'Yes.' She could have stayed on a little longer while the newcomers got the hang of things, and she had been considering that until yesterday had changed her mind. 'My job's finished, everything all right with you?'

He always said he was fine when she spoke to him on the 'phone but now she looked at him, quietly and dispassionately, and was shocked at the difference the summer had made. He wasn't looking well. His face was thinner and there were lines that she could hardly remember before. He didn't look boyish any longer and his grin was wry although he said, 'Everything's all right.'

'I don't believe you.' She came out of the kitchen, her

eyes fixed on his face. 'You're looking rough. You're not ill are you?'

'Of course I'm not.' He finished the whisky, and looked at the cupboard as if he was considering another. 'Business isn't so great,' he said.

There were people in the centre. This was a busy tourist town. Even as late in the season as this the streets were crowded and the car-parks were full. But that didn't mean the traders were making a fortune and Morag had no real idea how the antique centre was faring. She knew that she had never seen Alistair looking so down in the mouth. She said, 'I'm sorry, but I'm glad I came.'

She didn't know what she could do, but she was strong and young and at the very least she could see that he ate his meals and try to make him cut down on the hard stuff. Stiff whiskies mid-day were going to solve nothing. 'You need a woman around,' she said. 'Where's what's-her-name?' Alistair's girlfriends changed so rapidly it wasn't always easy to remember their names.

'That was a very expensive lady,' he joked. 'I'm on the lookout for an economy model.'

'Things can't be that bad.'

'Oh but they are.'

'So there's no chance of me getting a temporary job here?'

'You? Here?'

'I wouldn't mind getting out of London for a while. I thought I might stay with you.'

'Well we could certainly use a stand-by. When they're out buying or need a day off they look after each other's units, but if you were here they could call on you. That could work out very well, and of course you can stay here.'

'Sure? I'll be no trouble.'

'Of course you won't.' They had a joke, that she was

the bad penny and he was the one she turned had never really been a trouble to him. Exc early days, after their mother had insisted o Calla and Morag had thought that her h breaking, he had worried about her then. But months, she was adapting. That was over nin ago and she had never gone back to the islan childhood was only a memory now. 'Drink your and I'll introduce you around,' he said.

She had met some of the dealers on an earlier twelve months ago, but there had been changes, s were strangers. This was a house like a rabbit war innumerable small rooms opened up for its present r and Alistair took Morag along the galleries and into alcoves and everyone said how alike they were a everyone seemed pleased to see her.

She could start work right away, minding the boo unit, the man who owned it was out at an auction, that an hour after she had walked into the building was discussing the beauties of an early *Ingol Legends* with an eagle-eyed old man and trying to s knowledgeable.

She couldn't go wrong, everything was p although when he asked for a trade discount he' her and the man in the next section had to come rescue, haggling on his absent colleague's behalf end eagle-eyes went off to think about it, but sell a *Lady Audley's Secret* and a nineteen-thir *Tim's Annual* during the afternoon.

Alistair was in the office most of the time ar chatted to the dealers around her. They friendly crowd. When she asked how busines all said up and down, none of them particularly worried, but when she mention brother was looking tired they agreed wit seemed fond of Alistair and concerned abo

Of course the overhead responsibilities

Tomorrow she would shop for food. Now she opened the fridge and found half a bottle of milk, and half a packet of bacon that had begun to curl at the edges. The cooker didn't look as though it was much used, and the few tins in a cupboard had flecks of rust mottling their bases.

After six o'clock she would be lucky if she could find a shop open, so it could be the tinned soup unless Alistair had a better idea. She put on the kettle and turned on the television and sat down, shoes off and feet up, on a green plush Victorian sofa, waiting for the kettle to whistle or Alistair to arrive, and watching the news.

He opened the door as the kettle came to the boil and Morag jumped up and went into the kitchen to silence it. From there she called, 'Don't you ever eat?'

'Of course I do.'

'I can't find much sign of it.'

'Out mostly.'

'Are you going out tonight?'

At least there was tea and coffee. She made tea for a change, putting teabags in two eggshell china cups, sniffing the milk bottle finding, to her relief, that the milk was not sour He said he had been going out but he'd called it off. He would go and buy some food and they would have an evening in together, just like old times.

'Very old times, my laddie,' she said smiling.

They had had meals together over the years, met and talked and gone their separate ways. But the last time they had shared a home had been on Calla, in a white-washed fisherman's cottage, nestling on the hillside high above the bay.

This was a very different place, a very different life. She brought in the tea and he took a cup from her. She sat down again on the sofa with hers. 'I've unpacked and moved in, is that all right?'

'Of course. Was that all your baggage?'

'How long am I staying?'

'As long as you like.'

He was glad to see her. She had hoped he would be but he could have had someone else living here, or it simply might not have been convenient for him to have a sister moving in. She had been prepared to look for digs while she looked around for work, but suddenly, yesterday, she had wanted to be with her family and that was her brother. She said 'There are two more cases. I've friends who are coming past here over the weekend, they'll drop them off for me.'

Last night she had packed most of her clothes, leaving the rest to be shared between her flatmates. She had never acquired much in the way of belongings, she had lived in furnished rooms ever since she left Calla.

'Shall I go out and shop?' she offered. 'You look all in.'

'Do I?' He put down his tea, untouched, on a round rosewood table. 'You're not far wrong there.'

'Sit down,' she said. 'Just sit, and I'll be back.' And then he smiled and that made him look better.

'No, I know what's open. You lay a table. Help yourself to a drink.' He took a plastic carrier bag out of a drawer in the kitchen. 'Don't go downstairs, I set the alarm on the lower floors when I go out.'

She opened drawers until she found the cutlery, then she set out knives, forks, spoons and dinner mats on the rosewood table. She didn't want alcohol on an empty stomach, later over a meal perhaps, so for now she went on drinking her tea.

Alistair had left the door open. Beyond it the top storey was full of shadows, the only visible light coming from the floor below. She stood in the doorway, holding the china cup and saucer with its delicate pink and gold tracery, and memories stirred in her of the castle on Calla when she was a child.

Once a month her mother had gone up there to help

with the sewing, mending usually, and sometimes she would take Morag with her. The child was allowed to wander but not touch and this was how the castle was furnished, all this period stuff. Morag had thought it was lovely.

It was very still. The sound of the television followed her a little way as she wandered among the furniture displays, stopping to admire a Georgian writing table. A lady's desk, small and elegant, there should surely be a secret drawer somewhere to hide the love letters. She thought, if I ever strike it rich this is the kind of thing I might buy.

She laughed at herself and saw herself in a mirror, startled for a second by the unexpected glimpse of a pale face and a mass of dark hair, then recognising her own reflection. The glass was flawed slightly, with age spots. The room made a vast shadowy background as she peered into the mirror. Then her eyes moved a fraction although she kept her head still, as though she half expected to see another reflection of somebody standing close behind her, looking over her shoulder.

She jumped so that the teacup jiggled in her hand. Of course there was nobody there, but it was spooky out here and she had hardly eaten all day. Not much from midday yesterday now she stopped to think about it. She was getting lightheaded and she could easily have dropped that cup.

She went back into the apartment. On the television a gloomy looking politician was droning on about nothing getting better, and she said, 'Ah shurrup,' as she pressed the button on him. That didn't make the troubles of the world go away but she had enough troubles of her own right now.

I will not think about Kevin, she thought. I won't be bitter, I won't be sad. There's plenty for me to do here, minding the stalls, and Alistair is needing somebody and this is my chance to give back a little.

There was another mirror in here, an oval glass in a narrow rosewood frame, hanging on the wall. The flame red of her hair and the green of her eyes were clearly reflected because in here the light was brighter, but she was scowling with determination and her jaw was set, and she grimaced and then grinned. Smile, she ordered herself, don't let him see you looking like that.

Alistair came back with a loaded carrier bag. He had been to a supermarket and to a fish and chip shop, and there was plenty here for tonight's supper and tomorrow's breakfast.

They sat down, with fish and chips on beautiful plates, and Morag said, 'This is all gorgeous stuff. Are these plates very valuable?'

'Victorian. They're not worth a fortune. About the same as good modern china. They're not mine, they go with the apartment like the furniture.'

'Well they're certainly very pretty. It gives me an appetite just seeing the food on them.' She wasn't hungry. She was forcing herself to eat and pretending not to notice that Alistair was not making much of a meal.

'You changed your mind about staying on at the florist's,' he said. 'Didn't you say they wanted you to?'

If she had found him how she expected she might have had a little moan here. But as it was she made a joke of it, 'You know it's a family that bought it. Mother, father, daughter and daughter's husband. Well Ralph, that's the son-in-law, has wandering hands and bad breath. He got me backed up against the chrysanths yesterday and I didn't fancy dodging him for the next two months, so I crowned him with a garden gnome and resigned.'

Her brother chuckled. 'Doesn't he know what red hair means?'

'Maybe he's colour blind.'

'What did Kevin have to say about this?'

Alistair had never met Kevin Sanders but Morag had mentioned him in her 'phone calls, because for most of this year Kevin had been the man in her life. Her exit from the flower shop had not been quite as dramatic as she was pretending. Ralph had grabbed her and kissed her, and he was not an appetising man and she might well have hit him with something, if his wife had not come into the shop at that moment so that he lurched back looking the picture of guilt.

It had all been rather revolting and Morag had walked out. She had been on her way out anyway, it was her lunch hour, but instead of going to the sandwich bar round the corner for her usual midday snack she had caught a bus to Richmond and Kevin's flat.

She said now, 'Not a lot. I broke up with him.' Alistair's affairs never lasted, and she smiled as she spoke so he let that go and refilled his wine glass, and she said, 'Now tell me something about the dealers. Start with the first stall and go round.'

She listened intently. She wanted to know about these men and women with whom she would be working, and to keep the image of what had been waiting for her in Kevin's flat out of her mind . . .

They hadn't even locked the door. It opened as she touched it. She had wanted to tell him why she wasn't going back to the shop and have him share her resentment in a cleansing blaze of anger. Ralph's mouth slobbering on her cheek had left her feeling unclean, and Kevin's touch would have wiped that out.

But he wasn't alone. He was in bed with a girl and his face, when he shot up from the sheets on seeing Morag, was as similar to Ralph's when his wife walked in as a handsome man and an ugly man could be. Talk about brothers-under-their-skin she thought, as she got out of the flat and the building as fast as her legs would carry her.

She hadn't stopped for breath, she had really covered the ground, until she reached Richmond bridge with the river flowing beneath. Then she had stood for a few moments before she walked on to the bus stop, looking down at the water. She had no urge to throw herself in but she did feel that she might very easily be sick.

Well it was behind her now. Kevin had 'phoned her flat that night and she had told him in no uncertain terms that she was through and on the move. She had tried to get in touch with Alistair but that 'phone had rung unanswered, and now she was here, and strangely everything could have happened for the best, because for the first time in her life Alistair seemed to need her. His account of his colleagues covered most of the meal. Afterwards they sat with coffee and brandies. He was drinking heavily. She hadn't known him to have a drinking problem, and he could hold it, it didn't seem to be affecting him, but it was surely another proof that all was not well.

As he poured out his third brandy while she was still fingering the glass containing her first, she said, 'This place seems fairly busy, I shouldn't have thought it was losing money. What is happening?'

'What happened,' he said, staring down into his glass, 'was that the old fellow died.'

She didn't follow at first, then she remembered. 'You mean the laird?'

This was Maconnell property and the Maconnells were the lairds of Calla. Alistair had worked for them ever since he left the island. They had a wide range of business interests and the old laird had been an easy-going employer.

He was a good man. Morag remembered him with affection, and when she had read the report of his death in the newspapers she had been sorry, but she hadn't expected it to alter anything. Another Maconnell would inherit. Callum. She remembered him too. She hadn't thought it would affect Alistair and when she 'phoned him next day and said, 'I was sorry to see the old laird died,' Alistair had said he would be missed and it had come as a shock. He had been a hale and hearty old man, the kind you expect to go on for ever.

That was all. They hadn't talked about it again, and now she asked, 'What difference did it make?'

'Callum,' said Alistair, 'is a bastard.' He grinned faintly. 'Not legally of course, more's the pity, but since he inherited it's been like having an axe swinging over your head. You never know when the chop's coming.'

'That sounds terrible.'

'Yes,' he agreed.

'But can he do it? You've worked for them for years. Aren't you protected?'

He gave a mirthless laugh. 'Protected? Against Callum Maconnell? They were pirates about three hundred years ago weren't they? If he isn't still flying the skull and crossbones he damn well ought to be.'

'Dinna fret my bonny lad,' she said, 'we'll ha'e him on the rocks between us.' She really hadn't a clue what Alistair could do if the man at the top was determined to make him redundant, she was just trying to lighten the gloom; and she tossed back her hair, her eyes glinting and her lips curved in a siren smile.

Alistair tried to laugh. Then he took another look at her. 'It's a funny thing,' he said. 'I suppose I still see you as the gawky kid who used to go barefoot. You were something even then, but you've grown into a girl who could stop the traffic.'

'I do it all the time. It's the hair. They think it's a traffic light.' She was anxious to keep him smiling and they reminisced about the days when she was gawky and often barefoot, and they had lived on Calla, until it was getting late and she had to say, 'Do you mind if I go to bed?'

She had no idea when he turned in. She had only

managed an hour or two of sleep last night, she had cared deeply for Kevin and she had been badly hurt. But tonight exhaustion claimed her soon after her head touched the pillow and she woke at her usual time of seven-thirty.

She came out into an empty room, went into the bathroom, dressed and applied her usual make-up. The kettle was cold so Alistair was probably still in bed, and she put it on to boil before she tapped his door to ask if he wanted tea or coffee.

When she got no answer she opened the door and he was still sleeping, under a huddle of bedclothes. In sleep his face seemed puffy, features coarsened, and she touched his shoulder and he opened sluggish eyes. 'Tea or coffee?' she asked.

'Coffee. Black.'

She was sure he had gone on drinking after she had left him. She didn't need to look for the empty bottle, and she didn't expect him to eat breakfast. But she scrambled eggs on toast, less greasy smelling than bacon, and set down the plates; and when Alistair emerged after a wash and shave the puffiness had subsided, leaving his face thinner again, almost haggard.

The dealers started arriving at half-past-eight, through the side door. Until then the building was empty, and Morag went down with Alistair and sat in the office while he went to collect the mail from the wire-mesh container behind the front doors.

He brought back a stack, slotting it into cubby holes in the office, and was left with five or six that were obviously addressed to him. Morag swayed herself gently from side to side in the swivel chair behind the desk and watched him open them, tearing the envelopes open one after the other, giving the contents a quick glance and going on to the next. He was frowning all the time until he opened the last, and then she saw him relax and she knew that a letter he had been dreading had not arrived.

She almost asked, 'Expecting to hear from Callum?' but she felt she must not try to force confidences. He knew she was ready with her support any time he needed her. 'What shall I do?' she said. 'I want to make myself useful.'

'I know,' he said, 'and I've got a feeling you could turn out to be my lucky charm.'

'Makes a change from the bad penny,' she said.

She worked hard that week. She moved from stall to stall, standing in for anyone who asked. Her looks and her warmth caught the customers and she made friends with the men and women who ran the stalls, and each day she thought that Alistair was looking a little less strained.

She worked on that. She saw that he had breakfast each morning, and insisted that he didn't feel he had to stay in with her in the evenings. His social life seemed brisk as ever, he went out most nights, and she got invitations herself. She was asked round for suppers, and on Saturday night she was going to a party at the home of the bookman and his wife.

Her cases had arrived today, dropped off by the couple who were driving from London up north, so that the small cupboard in the small bedroom was full now, and she had quite a selection of clothes.

She had decided to dress up. The clothes she had brought with her had all been casual, but this was a birthday party and it would be nice to sparkle a little. She put on a little black number that went well with her flame of hair, and rooted through her jewellery box.

It was all fake and fun. She had an 'emerald' set, earrings and a green glittering stone hanging on a thin gold chain. The dress had a low neckline and the 'emerald' glowed against her skin.

She was looking at herself in the mirror on the wall

of the apartment, fumbling with the little ring fastener of the chain at the back on her neck, when someone said, 'Still trying them on for size I see,' and the reflection of a man's face materialised just behind hers. She had heard nothing. A record of Shirley Bassey had been playing on the music centre and she had been humming along with that, but he must have come up here as silently as a panther. She was caught in a frozen moment, staring at the mirror unable to turn and face the man, because it was like slipping back in time.

She had been wandering through the corridors of Calla Castle, and had gone into the bedroom. The door had been open. She hadn't meant to touch a thing. It was a lovely room, she had just wanted to look, but a pearl choker necklace, milky as moonbeams, lay on the dressing table, and she had held that round her neck, admiring herself in a mirror.

As she stood there Callum Maconnell had appeared in the doorway. She had seen his reflection and dropped the pearls. It had been nine years ago but now she felt the same hot blush scald her cheeks, although this time there was no reason at all for feeling guilty.

He had hardly changed. He was a tall man, in his thirties, dark brows and a thatch of dark hair.

'What are you doing here?' she heard herself ask.

'How did you get in?'

'I own the place. I have keys. Is your brother here?' She was surprised he remembered and recognised her.

'No, but he shouldn't be long,' Alistair was collecting his car from a friend in town who had serviced it for him.

'I'm staying at the Swan. Tell him I'm waiting to see him.'

'Can't you wait here?'

'No.' She could sense the impatience in him. She bet he never adapted himself a jot to suit another's convenience, and she was so sure he was going to give

Alistair a hard time that she could hardly bear to breathe the same air. She wanted him out of the room and it would make no difference whether she antagonised him or not because his mind was made up before he came here. He *did* look like a pirate, about to order someone to walk the plank. She had thought long ago that he was the one whose black visage cropped up in the old family portraits. When he was at Calla in those days his path and hers had rarely crossed, but she would never forget him.

She said, 'Won't tomorrow morning do?'

'No.'

'It's just that we're going to a party tonight.'

'The party,' said Callum Maconnell, 'is over.'

After that she turned off Shirley Bassey—*Big Spender* was not a song she felt like listening to right now—and waited for Alistair in the silence that settled on her like a heavy cloud. This was going to be grim, it was what her brother had been dreading. Worse probably, he had been waiting for a letter but the man had come in person.

Perhaps the letter had arrived, or a 'phone call, because today Alistair had been sunk in gloom again. Until today she had thought his depression was lifting, but he had been silent at breakfast and he was reluctant about this party tonight. Even when he went out just now to fetch the car he was talking about dropping her off and then coming back here himself and catching up on some book work.

If Callum Maconnell was here to fire him it would be a body blow to Alistair's pride as well as taking away his livelihood because, until now, he had only known success. She would have backed her brother against any man on earth, but Maconnell was something else. Fierce in a frighteningly restrained way, a veneer of civilisation over savagery. There was not much sign of the old laird in him.

I don't see either of us getting to the party, she thought.

It seemed a long time before she heard Alistair coming, like waiting in a dentist's waiting room, and there was no painless way to deal with what happened next. As soon as she saw him she blurted, 'He's been here.'

'Who? He knew who. 'Maconnell?'

'He's at the Swan and he wants to see you now.'

'Yes, well it would be now wouldn't it? We mustn't keep him waiting.' He was wearing dark blue trousers and midnight blue velvet jacket and a fine lawn shirt. He looked pale and handsome, hopelessness in every line of his face as though he had received a death sentence.

'He can't kill you,' she said.

'Can't he? The Swan you say, I'll get round there.' His speech was slow and deliberate. 'About this party . . .'

'I'll 'phone, and make some excuse.'

'Yes,' he said, 'yes that might be best. You'll be all right then?'

'Of course I will. You think he's going to fire you?'

'What? Oh yes.'

'Well it's not the end of the world if he does. If he can. What can he do for heaven's sake?'

Alistair was not listening. He had cut off from anything she was saying, and there was more to this situation than the simple fear of losing his job. He wasn't even going to fight for it. Alistair had always been a great one for knowing his rights, nobody pushed Alistair around, but Callum Maconnell had already knocked the fight out of him. There had to be more to this than business not being 'too great'.

She would hear when he came back. Sitting around, wondering and worrying, would only give her a splitting headache. She had to keep moving and occupied. She had to *do* something.

She 'phoned the party-givers and said that Alistair had had a business call and she was dreadfully sorry but she had suddenly gone down with a migraine. It didn't matter to Morag whether they believed her or not because more momentous things were happening. Her brother had gone to meet a man who had said the party was over and him Morag believed.

She took off her little black dress, and got into jeans and a loose sweater, and started to clean the apartment. It didn't need it. Twice a week the cleaning lady did that, and since Morag had arrived she had kept everything tidy. But now she scrubbed the kitchen floor, emptied and cleaned out the cupboards, polished the floorboards in the living room and all the furniture until everything was gleaming like glass. Then she started on the dormer windows with their diamond-shaped panes, doing each tiny section at a time, and peering through them to the streets below.

She saw Alistair's car turn into the parking lot and she took the cleaning materials back into the kitchen, washed her hands at the sink, and went back to the living room. She sat down on the sofa and waited for him. He didn't look her way after the first glance, but he sat down himself and said, 'I'd better tell you about it.'

Then he was silent as though the words wouldn't come, until she said gently, 'He wants you out?'

'He wants me in jail.'

So it was that bad and telling wasn't going to make it any better. If talking would have helped of course she would have listened. Somehow Alistair must have cheated, fiddled the books, done dodgy deals, but his sister had always hero-worshipped him and he didn't seem able to spell out the details to her. She understood that. It was sad and sordid and looking at him now was breaking her heart.

She came and knelt beside him and put a hand over

his hand. 'I don't care what you did, I'm on your side.'

Her voice was gentle.

He looked at her then and his face crumpled as though he was in pain. 'I thought you were bringing me luck when you came,' he said. 'At first I thought you were.'

'I wish I could have done.'

'I've been gambling. Horses and the casino. I thought I might have something to offer him. I had a few good nights after you came but last night . . .' He shook his head.

She almost said, 'That was a damn fool thing to do,' but she bit her lip in time because she had never been in this kind of trouble. If she had she didn't know what lunatic risks she might have taken to get out of it. She asked, 'What happened just now?'

'He's coming here tomorrow. He wants all the books, the files, everything ready. He knows I'm in deep and by how much. There isn't anything he doesn't know, and he's going to throw the book at me.'

'Did he say that?'

'He's got a reputation for being tough as the devil when it comes to collecting his dues, I'll get no second chance from him.'

'What are we going to do?' It was natural to say 'we' because whatever happened to Alistair would affect her.

'You're not in this.' His sharp reply was a snub.

'In a way I am. You'd take on my troubles wouldn't you?'

'Yes.'

'Well I'm with you.' And a fat lot of help that was she thought, until he looked at her with a sort of dawning hope. 'I wonder, you wouldn't . . .'

'Wouldn't what?'

'It isn't fair to ask but if you'd back me up it might be some sort of excuse. If you'd say I've been helping you, that you've needed money.'

He was always generous with birthday presents and at Christmas but she had never asked for cash because she had never needed it, and she couldn't see Callum Maconnell considering her a case for charity. She said, 'I don't see what good that would do.'

'You're a beautiful woman,' Alistair reasoned and she would have laughed if it hadn't been such a horrible mess.

'You think I could spin him a sob story? If he's as tough as you say, and I'm sure he is, he isn't going to be taken in by the old hearts-and-flowers routine.'

'No, but he might not call in the law if you pleaded for me.'

Every bit of her revolted against the idea of pleading with Callum Maconnell. How on earth could she say that she had helped to rob him and now she was sorry and would he please forgive her? She shuddered, she would hate that.

She had just told Alistair she would back him to the hilt and now she seemed to be turning away. 'I'll think about it,' she said.

Possibly Alistair had spent money on her that was not his own and the least she could do was say how she felt about him, what a good brother he was and how crazy all this sounded. If any other man than Maconnell had been involved she would not have hesitated, she would have poured out her heart in her pleas, but he made her shrivel. And she was so sure that even if she went down on her knees to him it wouldn't make a blind bit of difference.

They pretended to watch television but neither of them did. Alistair drank steadily until bedtime, so that she gave up counting the glasses. She drank cups of black coffee although the last thing she wanted was to be kept awake. When he got to his feet just before eleven o'clock and wished her good night she said, 'Try to get some rest, it might not look so black tomorrow,' and thought what an idiotic thing it was to say. Tomorrow was doomsday, tomorrow was going to be the worst of all. Alistair gave her a little nod but again he didn't seem to hear.

She hardly slept, what with the coffee and the worry, until it was almost time to get up, and then she fell into a heavy slumber and woke minutes before they were due to start knocking on the side door to get into the centre.

She grabbed her dressing gown and rapped on her brother's door. No one answered so he could be downstairs but somehow she didn't think so, and when she looked in he was still in bed, still sound asleep.

She took the keys and went down, turning off the burglar alarm, and almost at once the dealers began arriving.

'Is your migraine better?' asked one of those who had been at the party.

She looked blank for a moment then replied, 'Yes, thank you.'

'Where's Alistair?' somebody else enquired.

'He'll be down soon,' she said.

In the apartment again she washed and dressed. She hated to wake him. With all this trouble waiting for him she wished she could let him sleep today and she closed his bedroom door quietly. He would wake before long. It was only a quarter to nine.

She would make the coffee before she called him. Her hands had not been too steady while she was putting on her make-up and they were still shaking. She stood waiting for the kettle to boil, her fingers locked tightly together and pressed to her lips as though she was praying. It had better be coffee, although she had drunk so much of it last night that she had an antipathy towards it this morning. In the end she made just one cup, and she had her hand on the latch of the bedroom door when the door into the apartment opened and Maconnell walked in.

CHAPTER TWO

DIDN'T Callum Maconnell ever knock and wait? Morag wondered and knew that of course he didn't.

'You again?' he said. 'Where's Macdonald?'

She nearly said, 'I'm Macdonald,' but he was not here to split hairs. 'It isn't nine o'clock yet,' she pointed out. He might have given Alistair time to prepare for this ordeal and she was annoyed with herself now for not waking her brother. She put down the coffee, aware that she was slopping it into the saucer, and asked with all the sweetness she could muster, 'You couldn't give us half an hour could you?'

'To my certain knowledge,' said Maconnell, 'he's already had two years and probably a good deal longer,' and with that, he opened the bedroom door.

Alistair hadn't moved, and standing in the doorway she saw the pills on the dressing table that she had never noticed before, and her heart almost stopped as she rushed across to grab the bottle. There were only a few left. It could have been full last night. She didn't know the name, she didn't know what he could have taken. He was breathing, he was alive, but he could be in a coma, it could be an overdose, and she glared at Maconnell with burning eyes and she didn't recognise the voice that came out of her mouth. 'If anything happens to him I will kill you.'

'Macdonald.' Maconnell bent over the bed and Alistair's eyes opened wide. He was not in a coma, but he looked as though he had been caught in a nightmare as he struggled up croaking, 'What time is it?'

'Up,' said Maconnell, and turned to Morag. 'I'll be back in fifteen minutes.'

'What are these?' She thrust the bottle under Alistair's nose.

'Sleeping pills.'

'How many have you taken?'

'None,' he said. The slam of the apartment door signalled Maconnell's exit. 'Why didn't you wake me, for chrissake? Fifteen minutes. God, what time is it?'

Suddenly active Alistair staggered into the bathroom. She heard the water running, and she heard him swear and presumed he had cut himself shaving and that his hands were shaking like hers.

She really had thought that her brother had taken an overdose, and she covered her face and for a few seconds, no longer, she wept. She couldn't allow time for tears. She had to pull herself together before the mist in her eyes made her mascara run. But it had been a horrendous shock and she thought crazily, if Maconnell comes back and finds me in floods of tears will that help Alistair? How pathetic does Alistair want me to be?

She couldn't plead for anything. She couldn't ask Maconnell for the time of day. She went into her little bedroom and took a suitcase from under the bed and began to repack her clothes. If he ordered them out of here she wanted to be ready to call a taxi and get off his property and out of his way.

Alistair had a piece of sticking plaster on his chin, and his hair was wet, slicked down as though he had dunked it in cold water. She said, 'Coffee?' as he came out of the bedroom but he shook his head. There were two minutes to go, she didn't think Maconnell would allow them much leeway, and she sat down on the sofa because her knees were rubbery.

Right on the dot he walked in, and Morag sat very still and straight. Arrogant swine, she thought, acting as if he owns the earth. He walked to the window and looked down into the street, then across at them as though he was waiting for them to say something. Alistair just stood there and Morag wished her brother would show some spirit and say something like, 'Get it over with. Whatever I've done there's no need to drag this on.'

'Well?' said Maconnell.

'Not very,' said Morag.

'You're a fine couple.' He was classing them together, and she glanced round at Alistair and wished she could hold his hand. 'I don't like being cheated,' said Maconnell.

'Not many do,' Morag muttered.

'You spoke?'

He'd heard and there was no point repeating it. 'No,' she said.

'Anything you want to say?'

'Nothing's going to help much is it?'

He sat down, in a chair facing the sofa where she sat and Alistair stood just behind her. She felt his scrutiny as though he had touched her roughly, and her head went back a little, her chin tilted up. He glanced at Alistair and then back at her and said, 'You're the younger aren't you?'

There were six years between them, and right now Alistair was looking older than his age. 'Shouldn't you be wearing glasses?' she snapped back tartly.

'No.' He had the most piercing eyes she had ever encountered, keen as a hawk's. 'But looking at the pair of you I'd put *you* down as the one who's been creaming off the profits, and certainly the tougher.'

Alistair was hangdog and she was defiant, and maybe she did give the impression of a girl who lived rich. She was still wearing the green earrings from last night and they might pass as emeralds. 'What makes you think that—the earrings?'

'No, it's in the eyes.'

'She didn't know,' said Alistair, his voice low, but

Callum took no notice of him at all and Morag had the
strangest feeling that this was between her and the man.

'But I've always taken from you haven't I?' Talking to
Alistair but still looking at Callum. 'You've spent
money on me and I just accepted it so I reckon I'm
owing as well as you.'

'What do you do for a living?' Maconnell asked her.

'Apart from accepting handouts.'

'I'm between jobs at the moment.'

'Resting?'

'I don't do much of that.'

'What do you do?'

'I've worked in a flower shop for the last twelve
months but that's just been sold. Before that I worked
in an art gallery, I was a waitress, I've done some
secretarial work and a few modelling jobs. I've worked
on the stands at exhibitions.'

'Quite a varied career.' None of which had anything
to do with him and he had better not try patronising
her.

'Like everybody says,' she drawled, 'I could write a
book.'

'I bet you could.' And that was no compliment. She
sat stock still and glared back at him, she wouldn't be
first to look away. 'I think you'll do,' he said, and that
made her voice rise sharply.

'Do for what?'

'You could earn him some time.' Callum smiled
grimly. 'I'll rephrase that. I'm offering you a job. Stick
with it through the winter and I'll leave him here.
There's nothing wrong with his work *if* he can keep his
fingers out of the till. He'll be paying me back of course
but it would give him the chance to come out of this
without a record.'

'Go on,' she said.

'You remember my grandmother?'

'Of course.' The ageing beauty who moved in a cloud

of perfume, dressed so stylishly with rings on all her fingers. She had seemed like someone out of a fairytale to Morag in the old days.

'You know what Calla can be like in the winter,' he said. 'It's where she and her sister are happiest but they have low boredom thresholds. They have to take life quieter these days and I want someone to keep them amused.'

'I'll take it,' she said and he smiled again, and this time the charm almost broke through the harshness.

'Tell them about your misspent youth,' he quipped. 'They'll like that.'

'When do you want me up there?'

'As soon as possible.'

'Does the ferry still run?'

'Still Wednesdays and Saturdays.' She could see it all again: the little bay with the bobbing boats, the shingle, the rows of houses. She could hear the piercing cries of seabirds and taste the salt air. Excitement stirred in her, and some other emotion she couldn't name.

'I'll be there on Wednesday,' she said.

'You'll be met.'

Morag went back into her bedroom where the case lay on the bed. She would pack her winter clothes into the two big cases and leave the lighter stuff here. It was Sunday today. She must book herself a flight to Glasgow for Tuesday, fix digs for Tuesday night; and on Wednesday she would get a train and then the car ferry to Calla.

After the strain of expecting the worst the relief was incredible. Alistair had gone with Callum but she had won him his reprieve, and the job she was being offered would suit her fine. She had weathered thirteen winters on Calla and could easily stand another, and it would be fun, living in the castle, and it would not be her fault if she failed to amuse Flora Maconnell and her sister.

She could hardly stop herself capering around and

whooping with triumph in the empty apartment, but Alistair looked grim when he came back. The last hour must have been an ordeal for him, and as he walked into the room he let out his breath in a long sigh. Morag, intending comfort, said, 'Well, it didn't work out too badly.'

'I don't know.' He slumped into a seat, and after a moment she prompted him.

'Well, what happened?'

'I'm staying here. I'm paying him back and he knows what I owe him. He's giving me time but——'

'But what? What more do you want?'

'It was too easy.'

'Why complain then?'

'It's where you stand in all this that I don't like. You remember the winters on Calla.'

She could certainly recall how the winds blew so that no snow settled although it was like breathing ice into your lungs. The storms crashed in from the Atlantic. She laughed and said, 'Sure I do but I'll be in the castle, which as I remember was quite luxurious. I don't mind being a hostage.' Perhaps she should not have used that word, although it was the right one. She started to say she was quite looking forward to going back to Calla. Alistair had always fretted against its restrictions, he couldn't wait to leave the island, but Morag had wept when she was taken away.

Before she could get out more than a few words Alistair said harshly, 'You'll be a prisoner.'

'They're not going to keep me in the dungeons.'

'So long as keeping the old girls happy is the only thing he's got in mind for you.'

'Do you think he fancies me?' And she laughed again because it was ridiculous. He had a very low opinion of her. The only thing between them was a clash of wills and personalities. 'He doesn't like me one little bit,' she said and Alistair snorted.

'I never said he did. I don't think he does. But I do know he never took his eyes off you. It was as though there was nobody else in this room but you.'

She had felt a little the same way but that didn't mean she fancied the man. 'He's a hell of a womaniser,' cautioned Alistair. 'And he's ruthless about taking what he wants. When he gets you up there how are you going to hold him off?'

Alistair was having second thoughts now, about throwing his sister to the wolves. Or the pirates Morag thought, and knew that she should not smile because it was very serious to Alistair. She was an attractive woman and there was a possibility that Callum Maconnell might think she was fair game. But he was no fool, his world was full of attractive women, and he was not going to risk force against a determined stand.

'I can always hit him with a garden gnome,' she said. 'Although they could be in short supply on Calla, so maybe I should take one with me.'

But Alistair was in no mood for joking. He was getting a break and it was due to Morag, but this job she had been offered was a funny business. It seemed to Morag that until she parted from her brother at Birmingham airport on Tuesday morning all the time they were alone together he was warning her about Callum Maconnell.

'I believe you,' she kept saying when he voiced his concern. 'But I'll be all right, I can look after myself.'

She turned at the checking-in desk to wave goodbye and Alistair was still mouthing, 'You watch it.'

She wished she could have reassured him that she was a big girl now and wise in the ways of the world. She would probably see very little of Callum, he might not even winter on Calla. And if he did have designs on her she had had experience in that kind of situation. She did not like nor trust him, and no matter how much sensual charisma a man had she would never lose her head over someone she did not like. She wished she could convince her brother that she was in no danger at all . . .

'Isn't it Morag Macdonald?' asked the woman on the ferry. Morag was standing at the rail, although the rain was coming down and the sea was a grey sullen swell. It was always like this in October, the October drenching they called it, but she had to be up here to get her first sight of the bay.

She had been homesick without knowing it all these years. That was why she had never wanted to make a permanent home anywhere else, because this was where she had left her heart. It hadn't changed. Her father's boat could have been among those drawn up on the shingle, her mother could have been waiting in that house on the hill.

She recognised the woman as Mrs McNeil who kept the store. Morag must have changed herself, from a skinny thirteen-year-old, and Mrs McNeil's smooth apple-red cheeks were seamed now with wrinkles, and of course there was no going back to the way things were. 'What's brought you back?' asked Mrs McNeil, and Morag asked at the same time, 'How's the family?'

Mrs McNeil was still giving her ten years' news as the ferry drew up in the harbour and Morag stepped on to the island again. She hadn't explained what had brought her here, and when Callum Maconnell came forward to carry her cases to the black Porsche that was waiting she was sure that Mrs McNeil would be handing out that newsflash over the counter to all her customers that afternoon.

Seeing him here had surprised Morag, although there was no reason why he shouldn't meet a ferry. She would have preferred someone else, so that she could have relaxed on the car ride through the familiar landscape. Just being near him made her tense, although he said nothing after asking, 'How was the journey?' to which she had replied tritely, 'Very pleasant.'

They were soon out of the small town around the bay and driving up the narrow track that wound its way to the castle. Calla Castle dominated the coastline, high and string as a fortress, cliffs falling sheer from its walls. Everything was supposed to look smaller than it did when you were a child, but the castle was exactly how she remembered from when she had trudged up here with her mother, and stopped at the lodge to talk to the lodge keeper's wife.

The lodge looked the same too, although nobody came to the door as they drove through the open gates. 'Are the Fergussons still here?' she asked.

'Fergus is. Sarah died.'

'Ten years is a long time,' she said quietly to herself.

'You never came back?'

'No.'

'Were you glad to get away?'

She had kept her head turned towards the window all the time, looking up into the rain-wreathed mountains, almost sitting sidewards to avoid touching him. 'I didn't have much choice,' she said. 'My mother wasn't born an islander. When my father died she only stayed a matter of days. I had to go with her.'

'And you haven't had much choice about coming back.'

'That's right.' They were drawing up now before the steps that led to the main doors with the intricate stone coat of arms above. It had always been a side door that had been her mother's access before. Morag had never had these doors opened for her in her life. She turned then to look at him before she scrambled out of the car, her eyes narrowed and her jaw set. 'But don't get the idea that I often get pushed around.'

'Do you think,' he said, 'you could look a little less pugnacious before you meet them? I can't see them welcoming somebody who looks as if she's spoiling for a fight.'

She was not spoiling for a fight. She was just telling him that she rarely got herself into situations of no-choice, and she said coolly, 'Don't worry, I won't walk in glaring.'

Goggling was more like it. She had always gone with her mother into the servants' quarters, and when she was allowed to wander she was expected to be unobtrusive about it, peering into rooms rather than marching around. First sight now of the vast panelled hall with its great staircase and heraldic beasts, supporting their shields, was impressive enough to make her catch her breath; and then two huge black hounds bounded out of the shadows and she took a hasty step back. But it was Callum they were welcoming, they took no notice of her.

They were Great Danes, the same breed she remembered here, although these were younger dogs; and the man and woman who came towards her had hardly changed at all. Hamish and Mrs Fraser had always seemed old and stern and disapproving to Morag. Mrs Fraser was housekeeper at the castle, stiff backed with iron grey hair pulled severely from a centre parting. She was a little greyer now, so were Hamish's whiskers and hair; but Morag would have known them anywhere, although there was no sign of recognition on their part.

'You'd better go to your room,' said Callum. She was wet and windblown and she needed a little time to make herself presentable. 'We'll be in there when you're ready.' He indicated a door that she knew led into a small drawing room.

'This way, madam,' instructed Mrs Fraser. She went a few steps ahead of Morag, and Hamish, carrying the cases, followed behind. Neither spoke and Morag was trying to memorise landmarks as she passed them because the corridors seemed to go on for ever.

When a door opened and the cases were deposited Mrs Fraser asked, 'Shall I unpack for you?'

'I'll do it, thank-you.' She pulled off the head scarf that had been knotted under her chin and her mass of wet red hair sprang loose and Mrs Fraser stared at her.

'It's never Morag Macdonald?' She sounded as though Morag had been caught sneaking in in disguise. 'Not Mary Macdonald's daughter?' When her mother had come here on sewing days Mrs Fraser had provided cups of tea and a mid-day meal, but there had never been any doubt about the social status. Mrs Fraser believed herself several cuts above a fisherman's family, and she wasn't happy to find young Morag moving in.

'Yes,' answered Morag, unbuttoning her mac. She was wearing a white and black checkerboard sweater, with a broad black belt and a plain black skirt, but there was style about her, she could have passed for quality.

Mrs Fraser sighed deeply and grumbled, 'I don't know what things are coming to. When he told me he was expecting a guest I never thought it would be Mary Macdonald's girl.'

I wish I could tell somebody about this, thought Morag. Mrs Fraser wringing her hands because the peasants are getting above themselves. It would send all Morag's friends into hysterics, they would think it was a scream, and it would be something amusing to put in her letters. It would have been nicer of course if Mrs Fraser had welcomed her with a smile but she couldn't remember that Mrs Fraser ever had.

She said, 'I'll put you out of your misery, I'm not a guest, I'm a worker.'

'Then what are you doing in this room?' Mrs Fraser demanded shrilly and Morag shrugged.

'I followed you. Would you like to call Hamish and ask him to put the cases somewhere else? Then I'll tell you if I'm taking it.'

'This was the room I was told to prepare.'

'Then sorry, but this is it. And now if you don't mind . . .' She put out a hand as if she would have guided Mrs Fraser out.

Mrs Fraser didn't wait to be removed but as she went she said, 'I suppose you're another friend of Mr Callum's, I don't know what girls are coming to. I'll say this for your mother, she was always a respectable body.'

It was obvious that Mrs Fraser was not considering Morag respectable. The way she had said, 'another friend of Mr Callum's' meant another easy lady, which was what Alistair had warned her against, and all she could do about that was keep setting the record straight.

This was a beautiful room, with its fourposter bed mushroom pink bed-hangings and a white lace coverlet. On the floor was a large blue and cream Chinese rug, and subtle shades of pink and blue featured in the floral patterned wallpaper. Not a room, Morag felt, that Mrs Fraser would have given to one of the staff unless it had been specified.

There was another door and Morag turned the knob to open it with a wry expression. When she saw a small and pretty bathroom the smile stayed wry but she was relieved about that. It could have been rather awkward if there had been another bedroom through there, and she wondered where exactly Callum's bedroom was, and hoped it was a good distance from her own.

She dried her hair, washed her face and put on fresh make-up, before she tried to find her way downstairs. First impressions counted, she didn't want Flora Maconnell deciding she didn't want Morag Macdonald hanging around all winter long. She couldn't see how Callum could get out of giving Alistair a second chance even if the sisters did take a dislike to her, but it would be humiliating. Besides, she didn't want to go back to the centre, she wanted to stay here.

She changed into a grey flannel suit and an emerald green silky blouse and left the rest of her unpacking until later. When she came out of her room the long corridor was empty. She walked slower now than when she was being marched up between the Frasers. She took her time and looked around and she remembered almost everything from her childhood: pictures, tapestries, pieces of furniture, the occasional suit of armour. The faces in the portraits went back over four hundred years and more than one had the Callum stamp.

She started looking for it: the eyebrows in this portrait, the mouth in another. You could always find something to interest you in a place this size, it would be like living in a museum. When winter really came and she couldn't get out of the castle much less off the island she could amuse herself by finding out who these people had been. She bet the Frasers had all the family history by heart, if they could bring themselves to discuss her betters with Morag Macdonald.

When she came to an oil painting of a heavily bearded gentleman in full regalia of dark green velvet jacket, white lace at wrists and throat, and the dark red and green kilt of the Maconnells, she stood back, arms folded, looking at him. He had dark eyes—another link with Callum—and he was scowling. Even the background was stormclouds, and she said, 'I bet you were a load of laughs,' and realised at the same moment that Callum was at the other end of the corridor.

If he had rounded the corner a second earlier she would not have been caught talking to herself. She didn't make a habit of it, most of the time she kept her thoughts in her head. But this portrait was a little unnerving and awfully lifelike.

'We wondered what was keeping you,' said Callum. 'Are you having a word with all of them?'

He must think she was mad. 'Just him,' she said. 'He looked the gloomiest of the lot.'

'I can see you're going to be a real ray of sunshine around the place but you don't actually have to chat up the paintings.'

'Why not?' she said. 'It's nice to meet a Maconnell who won't answer back.'

She couldn't help the impudent quip, although she knew it would be wiser to leave him with the last word. He had turned and she was following, and watching the tall athletic figure with its broad shoulders striding ahead she thought, I want my stay here to be peaceful and I want him to take as little notice of me as possible, so I must do something about whatever it is in me that does seem to be spoiling for a fight.

One of the great dogs was with him. The other lay in front of the fire that burned in the white marble fireplace. There were two women sitting in highbacked chairs, and on a footstool by one of them, sat a Skye terrier with a pink bow perched on top of its head. When Morag walked into the room with Callum all eyes fixed on her.

Flora Maconnell didn't look ten years older. Her hair had been softly waving ash blonde ever since Morag could remember, and her skin was still smooth and palely translucent. There was a painting over the fireplace of the two sisters as girls, alike and very beautiful although Flora's smile was the more provocative.

Sixty years had not altered her out of recognition. She was still girlishly slim and there were no lines on her face as though life had disappointed her. She looked, Morag thought, as if it had been roses all the way.

Her smile was gracious as she held out a ring-laden hand to Morag. 'Why my dear, how pretty you've grown. I remember you as no more than a child.'

Morag was surprised she was remembered at all. She had glimpsed Flora and her sister from time to time,

being ushered on to the ferry and causing a great deal
of fuss, or driven around the island. She had
occasionally seen them in the castle but Morag had
been very much in the background. Now Morag took
the proferred hand and wondered whether she was
expected to bob a curtsey. 'You're staying with us for a
while, said Flora Maconnell, 'to keep us out of
mischief, Callum says.'

'I can't place you at all,' Dora Maconnell said
suddenly.

She was Flora's twin, widowed long before Morag
was born. She was plump and billowy as a feather
bolster, with three chins to Flora's one, and a generally
vague air about her. 'It was a long time ago, said
Morag. 'My mother used to come up here and help
with the sewing.'

'So they tell me,' said Dora. 'I remember your mother
but I still can't place you.'

Flora patted a chair next to her. Morag sat, and
reached to stroke the black dog that was stretched in
front of the fire and both women warned her, 'Don't
touch that one!'

The Great Danes were fearsomely large but neither
seemed unfriendly. Not friendly either, they had simply
ignored her, and she looked at the Skye terrier that
promptly bared its tiny teeth.

She liked dogs. She got on well with them. Friends'
pets made an instant ally of her, and the dogs she
stopped to talk to in the street invariably wagged their
tails. 'Don't they like outsiders?' she asked.

She was an outsider here and the animals' animosity
emphasised that. 'Polly is spoiled rotten,' said Callum.
'And James and Henry,' he indicated which was which,
to Morag they looked like as two peas, 'answer to
Jekyll and Hyde. Hyde's the one who thinks he's a
werewolf.'

Those teeth, backed by all that muscle, would be no

joke. 'How do you tell when he's going to turn?' she asked.

'To the naked eye it isn't easy,' said Callum. 'Now I've got work to do so I'll leave you to get to know each other,' and the two old women turned to look at Morag again, with a directness that convinced her they knew she was here because her brother had been caught embezzling, and probably that she was supposed to have helped him spend the money.

'Now tell us,' said Flora Maconnell, 'where did you meet my grandson?'

'In the antique centre in Moreton Meadows. My brother Alistair is the manager.'

'Now he would be Mary's son,' Dora mused. 'I don't think we ever met him.'

Flora shook her head, as if the name was ringing no bells with her, and it was possible they didn't know everyone who was employed in the Maconnell empire. Nor that some employees had been lining their own pockets before Callum started vetting the accounts. Morag hoped they didn't. It would make her stay here easier.

Callum's grandmother was still giving her an 'old-fashioned' look. 'You and Callum are friends?' She said that rather as Mrs Fraser had and Morag flushed angrily, because everybody here suspected she was having an affair with Callum which was why he had brought her to the castle.

She was in two minds whether to tell them the truth, she almost felt she would prefer being classed as a crook rather than marked down as Callum Maconnell's mistress.

She said emphatically, 'No, we are *not* friends, just acquaintances. We met for the first time on Saturday and he offered me a job, making myself useful to you. The job I had was part-time and temporary and I was an island girl so I don't mind the winters here.'

The sisters exchanged puzzled glances. 'You don't

look like an island girl,' said Flora.

'More like an actress or a model,' said Dora.

'I have done some modelling.'

'And you want to come back here? And stay for the winter?' There was an ivory-handled walking stick hanging on the wing of Flora's chair, and she moved now, awkwardly shifting her weight, and Morag wondered if that was where the years had told on her.

They plainly could not understand why a girl with Morag's looks was prepared to winter on Calla as companion to two old women, and Flora asked, 'Why did you leave London? Was it a love affair that went wrong? Are you running away from somebody?'

As Morag started to say no she realised that *was* how it had all begun. Finding Kevin in bed with that girl had made her start running, bringing her here, and Flora and Dora took the shadow on the girl's face as an answer, and as they were both incurable romantics that explanation satisfied them.

'I hope you'll be happy with us,' said Flora, 'and I'm sure you'll be a help in lots of ways.' She looked down at her small feet in their expensive grey suede shoes with a sad little smile. 'I shall find a pair of young legs very useful and your mother was an excellent sewer I remember.'

Morag remembered the almost invisible darns in linen sheets and tablecloths, but she had no talent for darning, and although she had run up the occasional garment she couldn't see these two wearing homemade creations.

She said, 'I'm not up to my mother's standard but I can sew a little. I can turn my hand to most things.'

'Can you type?'

'Yes.'

'Then perhaps you could help me with my memoirs.'

'Or we could catalogue the library,' interrupted Dora hastily.

'They both sound marvellous ideas,' said Morag, and compared with the daring they did.

Then she had to tell them what had happened to her since she left the island. Nothing about Kevin, she wasn't telling that kind of thing, but about the jobs she had had and the people she had worked with and, because she had no regrets and most of the time, everything had been fine, it sounded interesting and racy and funny. And they both smiled as they listened.

Dora took her on a conducted tour. 'We don't want you getting lost,' she said, and there was more than a chance of that. There were doors leading to the disused north wing of the castle that were never opened, but the living quarters still seemed big enough for a hotel, and Morag was glad to have her memory refreshed.

Dora pointed everything out briskly, she looked vague but there was nothing woolly about her mind, and when they came to the library Morag whistled soundlessly. The walls were lined with books from floor to ceiling, the bookman from the centre would have thought he had walked into Aladdin's cave, and it would take longer than a few months to get all these catalogued.

'I've always thought it was a job that ought to be done,' Dora said, as if reading her thoughts.

On one of the higher shelves there was a long row of Victorian romances with lovely titles. Morag could remember climbing up the steps when she was a child and sometimes, very carefully, taking one out and looking at the pictures. She had never dared to risk starting to read one because she had no business touching the books.

'Well, I could begin cataloguing,' she said. 'I suppose it's like filing on a grand scale.'

Night fell quickly here at this time of year. One moment it was dusk, the next dark and Dora was turning on lights. She left Morag at the door of

Morag's bedroom and said, 'We'll see you downstairs for dinner in half an hour.'

Callum would probably eat with them and Morag had visions of the food sticking in her throat if she tried to swallow it with his eyes on her. It would amuse him if she started spluttering and choking and had to be thumped on the back.

She started to unpack, hanging her clothes in another cupboard, placing them in another chest of drawers, making another room her home. She would be here for the winter, it was going to be that permanent, and then she would be moving on again. And this time she would be more alone than she had ever been because she could no longer rely on Alistair. She would always love him dearly, but if she struck trouble in the future it would be no use running to him.

In a pocket, in one of the cases, was a packet of photographs. It had been there for the past three months and now she tipped the snapshots out on to the Chinese rug. These had been taken during a party at the flat and of course there was one of Kevin, smiling at the camera and Morag.

Some of her friends would think she had been too hasty, dashing off like that, that she should have waited and thought about it —after all one slip didn't have to end a relationship these days. Her flatmates had hinted that she should be more tolerant when Kevin 'phoned that evening, cursing himself and swearing that it had never happened before and wouldn't again. Anyhow, Kevin had said, it hadn't meant a thing.

But it had to Morag. In the space of a few days the two most important men in her life had let her down, and it would be a long time before she trusted another man. She said, 'Goodbye Kevin,' and put the photographs back in the folder and thought, I'm talking to myself again.

She was not anxious to go down. She did not want to

spend the rest of the evening in Callum's company and she was sure he would be waiting. She was so sure that the two women would be sitting in the high backed chairs and he would be standing by the fireplace, she could see him in her mind's eye so clearly, tall and dark and arrogant, that she was quite taken aback when she walked in and he was not there.

He didn't eat with them. The three women ate alone and there were only three places laid. It meant Morag could appreciate the food, nothing stuck in her throat and she kept up a lively conversation. If she had been put at the same table as Flora and Dora when she was a child she would have been struck dumb with awe, but now she saw them as two nice old biddies and she set out to entertain them. That was what Callum had ordered, 'Keep them amused,' he had said, and she told them tales that had them chuckling.

Back in the small drawing room she ended the evening by reading to them from a novel and at half-past-ten Callum walked in. She went on reading. She was in the middle of a description of a sunset and she was glad it was not the page before with the steamy love scene.

At the end of the paragraph she looked up inquiringly and Flora said, 'Thank you my dear,' and Morag closed the book.

'You have a delightful reading voice,' said Dora and she told Callum, 'we've had a lovely evening. Morag's been telling us all about her life in London and it's been almost like being young again.'

Hardly, thought Morag. You never lived a life like mine.

'Do you know why she left London?' said Flora, and Morag looked down at the book and wished that the floor would open.

'I could make a guess,' said Callum.

'She had an unhappy love affair,' said his great-aunt.

'That I wouldn't have guessed,' he said, and she supposed he thought that Alistair had sent for her. Callum would have known how recently she had arrived at the centre. He thought she was there to take the heat off, on offer as it were, and it had worked because he had put in a bid for her.

'So we must be very kind to her because she's a very brave girl,' said Flora, struggling to her feet. She walked slowly and carefully, she had an arthritic hip. She used her stick and took Dora's arm, although she had taken Morag's earlier in the evening. This seemed to be their bedtime because they both said good night, and the Skye terrier trotted off between them, and Morag went to follow when she was halted by a silent gesture from Callum.

As the door closed she asked, 'Am I off duty now?'

'Yes.'

'Then can I go?'

'Of course. You've done well tonight, they're usually bickering from boredom by now. But don't get them feeling too sorry for you. Don't get any ideas of collecting while you're up here. They'd be a soft touch for a broken heart but we both know there's nothing broken about you.'

'Nice of you to say so,' she drawled.

'Rock hard all through.'

She had known for a long time that they didn't come any harder than him and she sniped tartly, 'You should know shouldn't you? That's the way you are isn't it?'

'Don't ever forget it,' he said.

She got back to her bedroom with no trouble at all. Not missing the way once, and very fast. She didn't hesitate until she was inside her bedroom and closing the door, then she picked up a shoe that she had nearly tripped over and hurled it at the opposite wall.

Now he was accusing her of wheedling sympathy out of the sisters, and goodness knows what else. Before she left here he would probably frisk her luggage to see what loot she was taking away. He had her down as a good old-fashioned gold-digger, and that was rich when she had been a working girl all her life. He was the one born with a silver spoon in his mouth and he made her so angry that all hopes of a good night's sleep had been blown.

She had been relaxed and comfortable, reading to the sisters in that quiet room, and although half-ten was about two hours earlier than her usual bedtime she could probably have come up here and got ready for bed in a leisurely way, and expected to fall asleep soon after she climbed between the sheets.

Now she was so hopping mad that she caught herself looking around for something she could smash. There was no shortage. There were several pieces of china and her own make-up jars. She could smash a window or a mirror or an ornament, and after the crash—which would be really gratifying—she could start working out how to convince everyone that it was an accident because no way would she let him know that he could get under her skin like this. So instead of smashing anything she had better take a hot bath and keep telling herself to calm down.

The water was cooler than she expected, there was no lying soaking and she had to towel herself vigorously to get warm again. She got into pyjamas and into bed, but she didn't turn out the light—she knew she was not going to sleep.

Her mind was still racing and it was so quiet that she was sitting up, her ears straining to catch the slightest sound. She had forgotten the stillness that settled on the island at night. All those years of living in towns and apartments had made the noise of traffic, doors banging, radios playing, a lullaby to her. She never listened to it, it simply washed over her, but now she was as alert as an animal in strange territory.

She hadn't even brought a book. She remembered the library and she wished now that she had taken something to read off the shelves. A Victorian romance, you couldn't get much more escapist than that, and there was nothing to stop her going down and getting one.

She had a torch, she knew where the light switches were. She went through the route again in her head and she was clear about it, she could go straight there. She put on her warm cherry-red dressing gown, fastening the tie-belt, slipped on mules and took her torch out of the drawer.

She didn't stop to look at anything as she scurried along the corridors, keeping the beam of light straight ahead. If she let it waver she knew that the eyes in all the portraits would be following her and she could easily start imagining that the suits of armour were on the move.

She reached the library in record time and switched on some of the switches by the door. Enough for her purpose. The shelf was too high to reach so she wheeled the steps along, climbed up and started to read the titles. She remembered some of them, and she eased *Held in Bondage* by Ouida out of its niche.

Then the dog leapt for her. She hadn't seen it coming, either it had slunk up silently or sprung out of the shadows, but without warning it was there, rearing up the steps—she shrieked and lurched away, and screeched again as she went an almighty crash off the steps, banging the back of her head on the floor and knocking herself silly.

Jagged lights flashed, there was a roaring in her ears and she screamed, 'Get off you brute.' Through the flashing lights she saw Callum's face—it was he who was doing the roaring, 'What the hell is going on here?'

'Your dog——' she gasped, 'your werewolf.'

She wasn't going to be savaged but she had had the

fright of her life and she was badly shaken. When she tried to lift her head pain knifed her and she gave a little moan. He put an arm under her shoulders, helping her to sit up, and her head lolled against him. 'I nearly knocked myself out,' she croaked, and she stood up sagging, and he caught her as her knees gave way.

She supposed she would have resisted if she had had the strength—she didn't want him carrying her, she didn't need carrying—but she had had the breath knocked out of her, and she was being saved from something that could have been very nasty, so she made no protest, just closed her eyes and lay limp as a rag doll.

She was no featherweight but he was carrying her as easily as if she was a doll and she thought woozily, I'd better not get into a fight with him, he could flatten me with one hand tied behind him.

When he put her down she opened her eyes and he was bending over her. His features blurred as she blinked, then went sharply into focus, and she still couldn't breathe properly. She had gulped in air as he carried her but now an iron band seemed to be tightening round her chest. He was frowning, a deep line between the dark brows, and she could see the shadow on his jawline and upper lip where a beard and moustache would have grown. 'I'm fine,' she mumbled and wondered why she was feeling so peculiar.

'Sure?'

All her bones were all right, she was sure of that. She could feel a lump rising on the back of her head when she touched it gingerly, and there was a lump in her throat too so that she had to gulp before she could speak again. 'Well I will be as soon as I've got my breath back.'

'Everything all right?' That was Hamish Fraser's raised voice.

'Yes,' said Callum.

'We thought we heard screaming.' Mrs Fraser now. 'And a crash.'

'I slipped off the library steps,' said Morag weakly, 'but I'm all right.'

She hadn't raised herself to look at them, she couldn't start on excuses and explanations for the Frasers tonight. She shut her eyes again and listened to her own heart thudding away, until she was pretty sure they had gone, then she sat up.

She was in what had been the little reading-room-cum-study leading off the library. She lay on a leather sofa that she remembered and the big desk and the captain's chair, and the ancient globe of the world still there in the corner. But now there were cabinets and office equipment and it was obviously a working office.

The desk lamp was the only light on in the room, and there were papers on the desk. He must have been sitting there, jacket off, shirt open at the neck, when she crashed off the ladder, screaming.

'What were you doing down here?' he said.

'What would I be doing in a library? I came down for a book, I couldn't sleep, I'm not used to the quietness yet. Then Hyde jumped me.'

'That was Jekyll.'

'Now he tells me. Have you ever considered belling Hyde?'

'Not a bad idea.'

It would be a good idea if she got back to her own room, and she stood up, and this time her legs supported her. 'Do you want a brandy?' he asked.

Morag didn't think that would steady her. She thought it might have the opposite effect. 'No thanks,' she said and after a moment's uncomfortable silence, 'I seem to have lost my shoes.'

They had gone flying when she went sprawling. They

were lying on the floor in the library, and so was the book and the Frasers must have seen all that so they should know what had happened. Once Callum had retrieved them she stepped into her mules and Callum handed up the book and said, 'Good lord,' as though her choice surprised him.

'I remember the pictures,' she said, 'I thought I'd read the story, but now you mention it it *is* a pretty apt title.'

The two dogs were there and she still couldn't tell which was harmless and which was not, but she was in no doubt about the man. He was dangerous. 'Shall I see you to your room?'

'*No.* Thank you.' Her reply was definite. Her torch still worked. She clutched the torch in one hand and the book in the other and said, 'Sorry I disturbed you,' and walked out of the library without looking back.

She would be stiff tomorrow, maybe with the odd bruise and headache, but she could have fared worse. She got back to her room without any trouble and took off her dressing gown and plumped up the pillows. Then she turned the key in the door. She hadn't bothered before, she didn't know why she was bothering now because she was sure that no one was going to walk in.

When he had asked if he should see her to her room, it was only because a couple of minutes before she had been buckling at the knees. Of course he would have left her at the door. Anyhow she hadn't needed helping back, and she certainly hadn't wanted him with her, up the darkened stairs and along the corridor, putting a hand on her to steady her step.

My stars no, she thought. She switched out the light and got into bed, and she was almost asleep before she let herself start wondering how it would have felt to have touched his face when he bent over her. Following the shadow of the stubble, first with fingertips and then with tongue. The rough touch and taste would have been a very sexy sensation, and it would have been suicidal. She would never risk making a move like that but she had never denied, to herself, that he was sexy.

CHAPTER THREE

NEXT morning Morag woke with a large bump on the back of her head, but that seemed almost her only injury from last night's fall. She had twisted no muscles and she didn't find the other bruise until she was yanking on her tights. That injury was on her bottom so there was nothing to show, and once she had apologised to the Frasers she would be able to put the whole thing out of her mind. She could just forget the memory of Callum's face hovering just above hers, and the strength of him when he carried her. Those were the *last* things she should be dwelling on.

Grey light filtered through the window and through the steady rain, and she heard the hum of an engine and saw the helicopter rising into the clouds and there, she was fairly sure, went her jailer. It was unlikely that anyone else would be taking off from the castle grounds.

She had a crazy impulse to open the window and wave. Maybe something white, a handkerchief or a towel, the flag of surrender. Never in a million years she thought, but the idea made her smile. The helicopter circled and flew over the castle to head, she presumed, for the mainland, and she turned away from the window.

The book that had caused so much trouble last night was unopened on her bedside table. In the end she had fallen asleep without reading a word, and now she looked at it again and went on grinning. *Held in Bondage*, what a choice to make, but the title was not a joke she could share. Alistair wouldn't be amused and nobody else had to know why she was spending the winter in Calla Castle. And now she stopped to think about it perhaps it wasn't so funny after all.

All the same, and in spite of the foul weather, excitement fizzed in her as she stepped out of her room.

She had only come up to the castle a few times in the years her mother had worked here, but this morning it all seemed familiar. She knew her way around as well as she would know the streets of the little town around the bay. She used to dream of the castle, that was why—she had lived in it in her head when she was a child.

She met no one now, through the labyrinth of corridors, down the stairs crossing the great hall and walking down the flagstoned passage to the kitchens. There was a little room off here where Mary Macdonald had stitched away on the first Monday of every month. That door was closed, so too the doors that led to cellars and sculleries and laundries, but the open kitchen door still revealed a room that seemed vast as a barn.

The huge open fireplace, festooned with hooks, hanging chains, spits and black iron pots had not been used since Victorian times. Mrs Fraser was preparing breakfast at the far end where there was a modern gas stove, and Hamish sat at the end of the long scrubbed-top table with a great mug of tea and what had been a large bowl of porridge.

When Morag walked in neither of them turned. Her footsteps sounded on the flagstones as she walked the length of the room but neither gave any sign of hearing her. They were listening to the local radio. The announcer was speaking in Gaelic. She hadn't heard a word of that in nearly ten years but it came back to her now, a birthday greeting and flowers to the girl whose name had come out of the hat.

'Máduinn mháth—Agus an duigh se Eileen Perry a tha faighinn na flúran oir is e ceann latha breigh a thann.'

'Morning,' Mrs Fraser's greeting was curt and

Hamish took a final swig of tea and strode off without a word.

'About last night . . .' Morag began.

'Next time,' said Mrs Fraser, 'we'd be obliged if you'd do your sky-larking *before* folk are in bed.'

If Morag started to laugh she would never be forgiven and she managed to keep her lips steady. 'I came down to get a book from the library and I was on the steps when one of the dogs jumped up and I fell off.'

Toast jumped up from a toaster and Mrs Fraser folded it in a white napkin. 'I suppose you knew that Mr Callum was in the office.'

'I didn't know it was an office,' explained Morag and Mrs Fraser gave her a you-must-think-I-was-born-yesterday look, then spoke again with heavy sarcasm.

'You might as well take up the breakfast tray, if that isn't too much trouble. Nobody's told me what you're supposed to be doing here.'

'Anything I'm asked to do,' said Morag, adding hastily, 'By the ladies.'

'And that's what you've come back for is it?' Mrs Fraser poured hot water into two glasses in silver filigree holders. 'At this time of year and looking the way you do?'

Morag almost said, 'I was homesick for Calla', but she didn't think that would be believed either so she just nodded.

'Do you know which room it is?' Dora had pointed to a door in the same corridor as Morag's and said, 'That's our room.'

'Yes,' said Morag, 'it's near mine.'

'And near the master's,' said Mrs Fraser grimly. 'You know that of course.'

'No——' Morag began, then she shrugged—this argument was a waste of time.

Breakfast for the sisters was two glasses of hot water

and lemon, tea, toast and honey. In spite of the egg-shell china the wooden tray was heavy and cumbersome. 'Take the back stairs,' Mrs Fraser ordered as Morag picked up the tray.

The stone staircase rose steeply, and Morag was negotiating the first bend when a dog came pounding up behind her from the kitchen. 'Whoever you are,' she said through gritted teeth, 'I'm on your side,' and he went past her, followed a moment later by his twin.

Mrs Fraser could have shut the door. She could have called the dogs back. Mrs Fraser would not have been displeased if Morag had dropped the tray, but six months as a waitress were coming in handy. Morag kept it steady and continued her climb.

When she reached the first floor the dogs had disappeared. The stairs went up and up, by now they could be frisking around on the battlements.

The room the sisters shared was the one Morag had walked into long ago when she had held the pearls round her throat to look at herself in the mirror. The door was opened now by Dora wearing a flowing pale blue fine woollen housecoat and blinking as though Morag had slipped her mind and she was surprised to see her.

Then she smiled and swooped on her hot water and lemon. 'Thank you, my dear. Would you put the tray there?'

'There' was a small table. Flora was propped up in bed against frilly pillows with her soft fair hair fluffed out and the tiny terrier sitting bolt upright at her feet.

They would see Morag downstairs in half an hour said Dora, and Morag wondered if she should be offering to help them dress or to fix their hair or to get Flora down the staircase. She was here as a Jill of all trades, but today perhaps she should just follow orders.

In half an hour she could go down to the kitchen and get herself some coffee, but first she went back to her own room and made her bed. She remembered empty rooms, and rooms where ethe furniture was shrouded in dustsheets, but there would still be a prodigious area to keep clean and tidy. She wondered how big a staff there was up here these days.

A door half way along the corridor was ajar and as Morag passed and hesitated a woman straightened from making a bed. 'You dinna remember me do you?' she said.

She was in her forties, fifties maybe, with a broad flat face and sharp eyes. 'It's Maggie MacTavish isn't it?' said Morag.

'Aye.' Maggie put her hands on her hips and stared hard at Morag. 'He's gone,' she said. She thought Morag was looking for Callum, and when Morag said, 'Who?' Maggie turned back to straightening the quilt, without bothering to answer.

'I suppose you mean Callum,' Morag said. 'I was just walking by on my way to the kitchen, I wasn't looking for him. I hardly know the man, we're almost strangers, and between you and me I don't much like him.'

'If you say so,' said Maggie.

So shut up, Morag told herself. Stop protesting so much because nobody is believing you.

Mrs Fraser was still in the kitchen, still listening to the radio and Morag got her coffee and a slice of toast in silence and then went into the hall and up to the first floor to wait for the sisters. This was a fantastic staircase, polished and gleaming, wide enough to take six abreast and surely hazardous for an old woman who was almost a cripple.

I'd have some carpet put down on this, Morag thought. It might not be in keeping but it would make it a darn sight safer. Or one of the downstairs rooms could become a bedroom. Surely that should have occurred to somebody, it seemed ordinary common sense.

She heard a 'phone ringing and a few moments later Mrs Fraser came into the hall, calling, 'Morag'.

'For me?' Morag ran down the stairs.

'He says he's your brother,' said Mrs Fraser. 'Take it in there.'

There was a 'phone in the little drawing room, on an ormulu table by the window. Morag spoke into it softly, her back to the room. 'Alistair?'

'Morag?'

'Yes of course. Are you all right?'

'Who was that I spoke to?'

'Mrs Fraser. You remember the Frasers. They run things up here.' She was almost whispering.

'Didn't sound very friendly. Do they all know all about it?'

'No, but there are several 'phones around so watch what you're saying.'

'Then what's the matter with her?'

'She always was an old battleaxe,' said Morag. It nearly slipped out 'and she thinks I'm having an affair with Callum,' but she bit that back.

'What's it like up there?' asked Alistair.

'Raining. It's October, remember?' He would know that was a month when the rain fell as though it would never stop, so that the boglands were black and the heather was beaten down. She could imagine Alistair shuddering.

'What a place to spend the winter. Everything is all right is it? I mean, is he there?'

'He flew out this morning. He's got a helicopter.'

'He would have. By the way Kevin 'phoned last night. Wanted to know where you were. Should I have told him?'

'*No.*' Morag turned as she heard the sisters come into the room. 'It's my brother,' she explained, and she told Alistair emphatically, 'I don't want Kevin knowing where I am. Not that he's likely to come all this way.'

He must have learned she had gone to her brother, and when she did write to friends in London she would stress that nobody was to leak this address.

'He's calling back tonight,' Alistair said.

'Tell him I did a midnight flit and you haven't a clue where I went,' said Morag. As she put down the 'phone moments later, Flora turned to her.

'Were you talking about your young man? Does he want to see you again?'

'Perhaps,' said Morag, 'but there's nothing to be said. It's very much over.'

Flora sighed. 'That's very sad.' She was leaning on Dora's arm and Dora settled her in her chair and hung the walking stick on the wing. 'Would it hurt you too much if we started on my memoirs this morning?'

'Why should it?'

Flora blushed a pretty rose pink. 'Well I suppose my whole life has been a love story. I've had such wonderful times, such interesting friends.'

She addressed herself to Morag while Dora sat down at the little bureau and made a great show of opening letters, ripping into the envelopes with a wicked looking paper knife.

'In that bureau.' Flora took a little key from a little purse, and pointed to an identical bureau. 'In the drawers.'

Morag turned the key and pulled the top drawer open. It was full of bundles of letters tied up in ribbon, photographs, programmes. 'Are you going to write a book?' she asked and Dora's eyes rolled ceilingwards.

'Just my memoirs,' said Flora. 'Just a record for future generations. For Callum's children.'

'Is he getting married?'

'If he was, surely the Frasers wouldn't expect him to bring a mistress into the castle.

'We hope so,' said Flora.

'Before long,' said Dora, nodding approval this time.

They probably knew something the Frasers did not know and Morag longed to ask, 'What's she like?' because she wondered what kind of girl Callum Maconnell would choose as a mate for life. Or had these two selected somebody suitable and were they just hoping it would work out?

He won't be pushed be the push ever so gentle, Morag could have told them. Tying him down would be like trying to cage a whirlwind.

The rain was still beating on the window panes and she longed to be out there. If she had an hour to herself today she'd go barefoot again, climb the rocks or run through the heather, with the wind and the rain in her hair.

'Morag,' said Dora anxiously, 'are you all right?'

'Oh yes.' Morag smiled for her. 'I was just thinking it's nearly ten years since I was on the island and that later, perhaps, I'd like to go for a walk.'

'In this weather?' both sisters chorused, and Morag had to smile again at the horror in their voices. She had been here less than twenty-four hours and look what it was doing to her already. Nobody in their right mind would want to go out walking in this.

'Do you drive?' asked Flora.

'Yes.' She hadn't had a car since rust got the better of her little banger earlier in the year but she could drive, although touring the island by car wouldn't be the same.

'You could take a car if there's anyone you want to visit. Do you have any family here?'

'No.' She had lost touch with friends and neighbours long since. She looked down again at the drawerful of memories and asked, 'How shall we start?'

She soon understood why Flora Maconnell was easily bored now that she was confined to Calla. In her heyday she had been everywhere and met all manner of famous folk. The men especially seemed to have been struck by her: artists, actors, politicians, tycoons, had written her letters, and Morag thought it was as well most of them were dead because some of this was highly personal stuff. She wondered if they had realised that Flora kept it all in a bureau that anyone could have opened, and what on earth her husband had thought about it.

Dora had probably passed sixty years disapproving of Flora's flightiness although as the photographs came out and Flora read extracts from the letters, and reminisced a little, Dora joined in. Morag made notes and wondered if she could get hold of a tape-recorder because this was a record of a by-gone age.

She left them after lunch. 'We rest in the afternoons,' Flora had told her, and Morag found herself wandering through the castle again, just as she had done as a child. It all came back to her, and she made her way to the ballroom. She had danced in here sometimes, alone in the great panelled room, imagining other dancers, musicians up in the minstrels gallery, the chandeliers ablaze.

There had been great parties in the castle in the old days, but all Morag had seen of those were guests coming and going. She wondered if Flora and Dora were still hostessing it, and what rôle she would be expected to take. Well in the background probably but she could handle that with amusement, and she wondered if the girl they hoped Callum would marry would turn up soon.

She went up into the gallery and looked down, hands resting on the oak rail, and she could almost see them: Callum with a girl, everyone else eddying around, giving them space because they were the stars of the evening. Like in an old movie.

What was it Alistair had said ... 'I do know he never took his eyes off you. It was as though there was nobody in the room but you ...' and there was something, electric and explosive maybe, but some sort of current between herself and Callum. So that she almost believed that if he had been down there, she could have willed him to look up at her, no matter who was in his arms.

Maybe she wouldn't stay in the shadows. She would wait on the sisters, make herself useful, but with her red hair and green eyes and the way she looked and the way she was she would be noticed by anybody coming to the castle. And they could put whatever interpretation they liked on her being here.

The hours passed as she wandered from room to room, and outside the rain came down. She put on a mackintosh and went out through the side door, into the courtyard. The doors of the old stables and coach house were shut. There had always been horses up here. If she had been a rider that would have been a grand way of getting around. As a child she had ridden bareback sometimes on the little working ponies, but she had never been on a horse in her life.

Nobody seemed to be about and she walked through the gardens, over lawns, rounding the north wing. From the outside it looked intact, rugged and towering like a continuation of the cliffs. Before she left Calla she would explore in there, some of the locked doors must open, but today she just walked and looked down into the bay, out over the sea, and came back with the rain pouring off her.

She hung her mackintosh to drip inside the door and met Mrs Fraser in the corridor. 'There's a bike,' said Mrs Fraser, 'if you want to go sightseeing.'

'Thank you.' A bike could be useful. Her reply seemed to nonplus Mrs Fraser.

'Only it's been suggested you might be taking one of the cars.'

'What are the cars?'

'The Porsche, the Daimler and the Range Rover.'

'Out of my league,' said Morag, 'And I bet Callum doesn't know his grandmother said I could borrow one. Thanks again, I'll be walking mostly.'

Dusk was falling when they heard the throb of the engine. Morag was sitting with the sisters, watching a play on television. They seemed to be absorbed, neither had spoken for half an hour. Morag heard the engine first. A few moments later Flora said, 'That's it,' and Dora said, 'Yes,' and they both relaxed as though they had been waiting and worrying.

'Don't you like flying?' Morag asked. 'I should have thought it was more convenient than taking a boat across.' While Dora was saying that she and Flora never flew Morag could have bitten her tongue, because she remembered then that Callum's parents had died in a plane that had crashed into a mountain on the other side of the world.

She could hardly have been more tactless but she had forgotten—it had happened before she was born—and apologising would only make it worse so she said nothing.

'Callum flies everywhere,' said Flora. 'If he didn't we shouldn't see much of him but when the weather's bad——' She almost looked her age then, trying to smile away her fears.

'This is a very silly play,' said Dora briskly. 'Is anybody watching it? Can you play chess Morag?'

Morag could after a fashion so Dora gave her instructions for finding the set, in a cabinet in one of the other rooms. Maybe Callum looked in on them while Morag was away, it took her a little while, because there was no mention of him and again they ate their evening meal alone.

Dora was an even worse chess player than Morag was and soon lost interest in the game and again she was reading to them from the novel when Callum walked in. Morag had got into the swing of the story by now and into the skins of the characters. She was managing four different voices nicely when Callum opened the door.

Nobody told her to stop when she hesitated. The dogs came into the room with him, and he sat down, making himself part of her audience, and Flora said, 'Go on dear.'

They let her reach the end of the chapter and then Dora exclaimed, 'That was much better than television. Doesn't she read well Callum?'

'Very dramatically,' he said. 'I do like the lady with laryngitis.'

That had to be the husky voiced nymphomaniac, Morag had done her particularly well. 'I'm sure you would,' she said, and both Flora and Dora chuckled.

Polly had been sitting on the footstool at Flora's feet, now as the sisters got up the terrier jumped down, and good nights were said, like last night. With Flora's hand through Dora's arm and with the terrier trotting between them the sisters went off to bed.

'How did the day go?' Callum asked.

'Fine.'

'You found enough to occupy yourself?'

'I get afternoons off. Is that all right or would you like me to muck out the stables or clean the cars?'

'Do what you like,' he said. 'Just keep them happy. They like you.'

He must have come in earlier and asked them that. 'I could get quite fond of them,' she said. 'Did they mention what we did this morning?'

'The memoirs?'

The bureau was closed now. There was no sign of the morning's work but Morag looked across at it and said, 'Some of those letters are pretty hot.'

'But out of date. No chance of blackmail I'm afraid.'

She almost flared that she was no blackmailer but he was smiling and she laughed instead. 'I can see why you thought tales of my misspent youth might go down well. He must have been a very easy-going husband.'

'They all grew up together, the sisters married brothers, they were all easy going but most of that was playacting, I doubt if she ever took a lover in her life.'

'All the same,' she said. 'It must be a comfort to you that you look like some of the ancestors.'

He grinned. 'And that my father was in every way like the old man.'

'My brother says you're a bastard.'

'And we both know why.'

'Dora is toning it down,' she changed the subject hastily because to start discussing Alistair would be a mistake. 'I'm taking notes and a typewriter would be handy. Your grandmother wants a record of her life and times for her great-grandchildren. Dora is adding bits of her own and it could end up as the diary of two Edwardian ladies.'

'That should pass some of the winter,' he said.

He was sitting, relaxed, the two Great Danes sprawled at his feet, and the mention of his children got no reaction at all. She heard herself say, 'They seem to have someone in mind for you.'

'Yes.' His reply was non-committal and again she was consumed with curiosity.

She stretched to stroke a dog, and if it was Hyde he didn't mind. A log on the fire shifted and threw up sparks—if she kept staring into the flames perhaps she could ask a simple question like, 'What's her name?'

But she looked at Callum first and the hard handsome face, unsmiling now, told her she had pried far enough into his personal affairs. One thing she was sure about. He would not be a tolerant husband. Whoever the girl was, she would be getting a man who would stand for no cheating, and Morag had better get off the subject. 'Don't you ever worry about the stairs?' she blurted.

'Why? Do we have death watch beetle?'

'I wouldn't know about that, but how does your grandmother get up and down? They're such a great flight and so polished and I know she's been used to them for years but she isn't as agile as she was.'

'There's a lift in their room,' he said and that was such a simple thing, she should have thought of it. 'And talking about falls, no ill effects from last night?'

'Nothing much.' Although she had been sitting with care all day. 'A lump on the head and a bruise where you'd expect.' He raised an eyebrow and she went on, 'Mrs Fraser offered me the loan of a bike this morning. By this time next week I might take her up on that.'

She pushed back her hair from her forehead. She had just rubbed it dry when she came in this afternoon, there hadn't been time for washing and setting. For years it had been a cascade of smooth deep waves, she had forgotten how it frizzed in the rain. Tendrils were tickling her face now and she smoothed them up from her cheeks with both hands and he asked, 'What have you done with your hair?'

'I took it for a walk in the rain.' She could have got enough exercise under cover in this mighty maze of a castle and she said, 'I know there's scope for walking in here——'

'But you felt you had to escape,' he finished the sentence. 'And last night you couldn't sleep because it was too quiet. It's a drastic change up here from the life you're used to, it won't be easy, but there'll be others around at the weekend, you'll have company.'

She thought of the girl again, that shadowy figure was beginning to haunt her, and asked, 'Anyone interesting?'

'Depends what you're looking for but don't get too excited. The average male age will be about seventy-five.'

'And that includes you? Whatever does that make them?'

'Very old friends of the family, but I won't be here after tomorrow.'

Good, she thought, I'll settle in easier if you're not around. But at the same time she felt her spirits sink and she asked, 'Aren't you scared I might ship out a few heirlooms if you don't keep me under supervision?'

'A risk I'll have to take.' It wasn't like last night when he warned her not to 'get any idea of collecting' while she was up here. She knew he still wouldn't trust her an inch, but there was humour in this sparring, and she could say, 'I'll bet you've got spies reporting to you,' and they were both smiling, although of course he had. Probably not here but in his business empire there were men who were Callum Macconnell's eyes and ears and that was how he knew what Alistair had been up to.

'Who do you fancy for it?' he said.

'How about Hamish? But if it's Hamish you should brief him. The Frasers don't know I'm a hostage.'

'Held in bondage.' He gave the words the leer of a melodrama villain and she gurgled with laughter.

'You make it sound very kinky. I think I'll put that book back. No, the Frasers think I'm here for the winter because we're having an affair.'

It was good for a laugh but she hadn't meant to mention it, and when the words were out she pulled a horrified face to keep the laughter going.

'It seems a reasonable explanation why I'm incarcerating a gorgeous female,' he said.

'And why the female is willing to be incarcerated.'

She was used to this kind of badinage, and so was he. It was just the superficial provocative chit-chat you could hear at any party. But there could be an element of truth in it. He probably could keep a woman here as a willing prisoner she realised with a clenching of her stomach muscles while he was telling her about the guests who were coming.

Two men and one woman. The Brigadier was an old flame of Dora's. Callum described them so that she felt she could recognise them and that it might be hard not to grin when she met them. She sat well back in her chair, listening, conscious of him as she always was, in every fibre.

He had an attractive voice, deep and slow and lazy when he was talking as he was now, as though she was a friend. His hands were brown and strong and his thick black hair was untidy and although he was lounging in the chair he still gave an impression of immense vitality and power.

'Tell me,' she said, when he'd finished his rundown of the guests, 'does anyone ever go through the locked doors? Can you get into the north wing?'

'You can but it's empty, there's nothing to see but stone walls. Have you exhausted the rest already?'

'Hardly,' she said, 'but I'm here for four months, I might want to go exploring.'

'Not in there.'

'Why not?'

'Because it isn't safe.' It probably was not and she probably wouldn't risk it although she might open a door and just look. 'That's an order,' he said curtly, and her expression was mutinous because there was no call for him to be so domineering.

'Sure' she said. 'You give your orders, I'm here to do as I'm told. Although explaining it wasn't safe should have been enough. Do you think I'm thick?'

'I think you're reckless,' he said. 'And you wouldn't be much use with a broken leg or a broken neck. So keep out.'

She did hate being bossed. She nodded and he probably took that for a promise. Once again she changed the subject. 'Are you going to be away long?'

'No.' She couldn't bring herself to ask, 'When *will* you be back?' She got up and said instead, 'Good night.'

He stood up too and for a moment she thought he was coming to her and her throat went dry.

Then he said, 'Good night,' but didn't move at all and as she walked upstairs she wondered how she could possibly have imagined that he was going to kiss her . . .

The visitors were just how Callum had described them. The Brigadier had a skin like leather, the colour of mahogany, a fringe of white hair and a small white bristling moustache, and he was still making sheep's eyes at Dora. Sir Charles and Lady Ensor both had high-bridged noses and a lot of strong yellowing teeth that made them look rather like horses, especially as she neighed when she laughed. Morag didn't see much of them. She was introduced as, 'Our new companion. Callum found her for us.'

'That boy always did have good taste,' said the Brigadier, stroking his moustache.

'By jove, yes,' said Sir Charles, and Lady Ensor looked down her aristocratic nose and gave a little whinny which could have meant anything.

They stayed for a week and most days Morag had most of her time to herself. She went down to the bay which was lashed by rain. The sky and the sea were black and sullen, and when she wandered into the General Store the three women who were gossiping with Mrs McNeil made a great show of surprise in recognising her as if it was the first time she had been mentioned.

'Staying up at the castle,' explained Mrs McNeil and they all nodded. 'My goodness you've come up in the world haven't you, hob-nobbing with the quality now.'

'I'm not a guest,' Morag said. 'I'm working there.'

'Aye.' They exchanged meaningful glances as she bought sweets and stamps and as she walked past the window she saw them with their heads together, and knew they were discussing the kind of work they imagined she was doing.

Years ago she had been a wild child and she remembered how one of the three had prophesied, 'Morag Macdonald you'll come to a bad end,' when Morag had cheeked her.

Now she was down as Callum Maconnell's mistress and, theoretically, that was going to the bad, although she bet that every woman in the island under forty, and a few over, were envying her.

She laughed into the rain and set off to climb the hill to the terrace of three cottages perched on the rocks, and the one in the middle in which she was born.

The doors and the window shutters were boarded across, there were holes in the roofs, and thin grasses growing high over the doorsteps. It was a depressing sight, because she had always imagined them as they were when she and her mother had left Calla. She had thought the neighbours might still be there, although on the one side they had been old and on the other there had been talk of emigration.

More than anything else these derelict cottages seemed proof that the past was dead, and yet as she had scrambled up over the rocks she had felt like the island girl she used to be. At least the island hadn't changed. That week she climbed mountains and wandered beside lochs and trudged over moors and gave up worrying about her hair, which was going to frizz so long as the rain kept falling.

Flora and Dora were happy enough while their visitors stayed, they didn't need Morag to amuse them. They went driving, cocooned in furs in the Daimler, all over the island. At home they talked about old times and old friends, played cards, and spent ages over their meals which Mrs Fraser prepared with great care, and which Morag helped to serve.

She ate most of her own meals in the kitchen. The Frasers were still stand-offish but Morag was the youngest of the staff. There were two other women who went home at nights, and three men working under Hamish. Morag was willing to fetch and carry, and Mrs Fraser was realising that Morag Macdonald might look like a lady these days but she wasn't expecting anybody to wait on her. In fact she was being quite a help now there were these old cronies of the sisters using the place like an hotel.

Morag started on the library, making a list of the books, and she had a 'phone call from Alistair who said that Kevin had been in touch and he had passed on Morag's message about a midnight flit. 'I don't know whether he believed me. I didn't tell him where you are, but I expect somebody will.'

She had made no 'phone calls and written no letters since she came to Calla. She was always meaning to write but somehow the days and evenings slipped by and she had no trouble sleeping now. Most nights she flaked out the moment her head touched the pillow.

'Is he still there?' Alistair demanded.

He meant Callum of course. 'Not lately.'

'Perhaps you won't be seeing much of him after all. I can't see anybody stopping on Calla in winter from choice and I don't suppose he's away long from where the money's made. The old laird's life wouldn't suit him.'

'He has an office here,' said Morag, 'I should think he could run things from here.'

'Are you doing any work for him?'

'Secretarial you mean? No.'

'So he didn't want you up there for that,' said Alistair. 'Although he's hardly likely to take you into his business confidence.' His voice was bitter. 'The only place he's planning on taking you is into his bed.'

Morag said sharply, 'I did tell you that anybody could be listening in to these calls. For God's sake show some sense.'

Not so long ago she could never have taken that tone to

Alistair. She knew he worried for her, she appreciated
that, but saying something like that on the 'phone was
very stupid, and besides she hated hearing it.

'Just so long as you stay on your guard,' Alistair
muttered, and she said, 'Yeah, yeah, yeah, and just so
long as you ...' she nearly said 'stop fiddling the
books,' she was that angry for a moment, but that
would have been unkind and instead she finished, 'stop
fussing because I'm fine. I'm cataloguing the library
and helping the sisters write their memoirs.'

Alistair gave a short sardonic laugh. 'What did they
ever do that's worth writing about?'

'Oh Flora had her moments,' said Morag. 'Could be
Dora did too, only she didn't keep the evidence.' She
mustn't quarrel with Alistair. He was all the family she
had and they loved each other, and no one was listening
on the line or she would have heard the click. 'But it's
all too out-of-date for blackmail,' she joked. Callum
had pointed that out and he had been joking.

'What I'd like,' Alistair said grimly, 'is something on
him. I'd give ten years of my life for a chance to crack
the whip there, and I don't care who is bloody
listening.'

He was still drinking, that was Dutch courage
talking, and the realisation filled her with sadness. She
wished she could have been near him to take the glass
away or at least try and she said, 'Are you still hitting
the bottle? There's not much point me keeping my part
of the bargain up here if you're making a mess of things
down there.'

'Don't nag,' he said. 'It's after hours, I'm as sober as
a judge all day, but I need a drink before I can ring the
castle. One of these days he's going to answer.'

Morag had picked up a 'phone as it rang tonight but
Callum could have done that if he had been here,
anyone could. 'Are you that scared of him?' she asked
incredulously.

'I've got this feeling that he's out to finish me just for the hell of it.' A whine of self-pity had crept into Alistair's voice and life had to be hard for him now, short of money and having to slog away to pay what he owed.

'That's nonsense,' she said, 'but if 'phoning here bothers you so much I'll ring you and report each week. Every Friday, about this time, O.K.? Goodbye then,' and she put down the 'phone.

She had taken the call in the library. She had been at the table when it rang, clipping another sheet of paper to her clipboard. Now she looked down the room at the closed office door. She had often found herself doing that while she was laboriously writing down titles and authors.

It was queer, this sensation that Callum was not far away. She could imagine him at his desk in there, and she half expected to see him in rooms or meet him at the end of passages. The dogs roamed the castle and the grounds—she thought she knew the difference now. Jekyll wagged his tail a lot and Hyde didn't. Whenever she heard them barking or came across them, she always expected Callum. And then of course there was the resemblance in the old paintings, long dead ancestors looking at her with Callum's eyes. He cast a long shadow, and it wasn't so much that she was constantly thinking about him, because she wasn't, it was more like a real physical presence, like hearing his voice and his step.

A few days later when she looked down into the hall and saw him below her she actually blinked to make sure and then he looked up. 'Hello,' he said.

'Oh, hi!' She hadn't heard the helicopter but the walls were thick and the windows were small, that could easily happen. Nobody had said that Callum was coming back. The guests had gone several days ago and right now the sisters were resting, and here was Callun in the flesh. She wasn't imagining him as she had done a dozen times.

She came to the top of the staircase and he waited for her. Being near him was like walking on the very edge where the cliff fell straight down to the rocks, if you slipped you could be over, and the danger exhilarated her, sharpening her senses.

All her attention was centred on the dark man. His eyes held hers as she came down the great staircase and she was almost on the bottom step before she even saw the girl beside him.

CHAPTER FOUR

She was a girl, not a woman. She couldn't have been a day over seventeen. She had huge harebell-blue eyes, long lashed, and she looked like Alice in Wonderland with her long fair silky hair held back from her face by a head-band. She was incredibly pretty and dainty and she made Morag feel seven foot tall and clumsy with it.

'This is Rosalie,' said Callum. 'Rosalie Perry. Morag Macdonald.'

'I've heard a lot about you.' The girl smiled, her teeth were as pretty as the rest of her.

'Not from me,' said Callum with a wicked grin that made Morag's lips twitch. She knew what everyone else was saying about her. Not the sisters but the islanders and the visitors, and if Callum hadn't bothered to reassure the girl it meant that he didn't much care if she got the wrong impression of what went on between him and Morag. So if this was the girl, she was the sisters' choice, not his.

It would be cradle snatching, Morag thought, and not his style, and it didn't strike her as odd that she should imagine she understood Callum when he was, in fact, almost a stranger to her. 'How's it going?' he asked.

'Fine. Were they expecting you?'

'More or less.' The three walked together into the little drawing room. 'They should be coming down any minute,' said Morag, their afternoon siesta was almost over. 'Can I get you anything?' she offered.

Rosalie had seated herself on one of the rose pink velvet sofas, Callum was glancing at a newspaper he had picked up. 'Not for me,' he said.

'No thank you,' said Rosalie, and Morag hesitated,

76

undecided whether to stay or go, then Callum smiled at her and she sat down. After a moment Rosalie said, 'You were born on Calla?'

'Yes.'

'We've been coming here as long as I can remember, staying in the castle.' She looked around the room as though she loved it. 'My father has a boat.'

The island had two harbours where yachts and deep sea cruisers anchored off shore, usually in the summer months. So had mine, thought Morag, and my father's father. They had fished for herring but the herring shoals had gone by her father's day. It had been crabs and lobsters that he brought back.

'Have we met?' asked Rosalie.

'I left here ten years ago,' Morag said. 'I haven't been back until now.'

Rosalie's lips parted for another question when Callum enquired, 'How are the memoirs?'

'We didn't work on them while the visitors were here, I started cataloguing the library.'

'You really are working?' Rosalie sounded surprised.

Morag replied promptly, 'Of course,' and looked at Callum with raised brows. He shrugged and it was a shared silent joke. She wasn't indignant about it any more, she was amused.

'Still getting out in the rain I see,' he said.

It had hardly stopped raining since she set foot on Calla. She had given up trying to tame her hair and become accustomed to the wild red halo. Rosalie's hair was the kind that would just lie flat and shining. Callum's black thatch would throw off the rain, strong and springing. Morag always got the feeling that electricity could generate from him, if you put your fingers in his hair in the rain you might get a nasty shock. The thought of it made her fingers tingle and she said hastily, 'I went home the other day, it was all boarded up.'

Rosalie said, 'Like the north wing you mean?'

The absurdity of that made Morag catch her breath then she said, 'My father was a fisherman. We lived in a little row of cottages and they are empty now. I suppose it's a sign of the times.'

'Things will be different soon though won't they?' Rosalie's glowing eyes were fixed on Callum as if he had the answer to recession.

'We hope so,' he answered.

Morag quipped, 'Don't tell me you've struck oil?'

'We're building a hotel in Stround Bay,' said Callum. That was on the other side of the island. In the summer there were campers on the hills, swimming from the white beaches. The old laird had discouraged holidaymakers, considering them intruders, but the sea could no longer sustain the island and the land had always been unproductive. A hotel would give Calla a summer trade.

'It sounds a marvellous idea,' said Morag. 'What's it going to be like?'

Rosalie began to tell her. Rosalie's father's construction firm were doing the building she informed Morag. She chattered on, bubbling with enthusiasm, and Morag thought, the winter will be over when this is happening and there will be nothing to keep me here.

Callum was lounging, as he usually did, well back in the chair not saying much, nodding from time to time when Rosalie appealed to him, 'That's how it's going to be isn't it?'

Morag thought, the hotel might keep me here. She asked, 'If you need a receptionist, a waitress, a barmaid, can I apply?'

'It won't be yet,' said Rosalie hastily. 'They can't start building till the spring.'

'Of course,' said Callum, as though Rosalie had not spoken, and his eyes held Morag's again with that intensity that blurred everything around, so that Rosalie's chattering seemed like a babbling brook.

You could keep me here, Morag thought, and she made herself listen to Rosalie talking about the hotel, show interest and ask questions, but all the time she ached with the strain of not looking at Callum. She had never met anyone before who could capture her senses so that everything seemed centred on him. And although he hardly spoke and she rarely looked at him, she felt that he never took his eyes off her.

Before long he was going to say, 'There's something incredible going for us,' and how could she deny it? Because this wasn't just good chemistry, liking someone, fancying them, feeling you might be good together. This was black magic. This man would be her lover because even if she said no, there would be no resistance in her.

When she did look across the spell grew stronger, and although Rosalie didn't seem to notice, Morag wondered if Callum did. She wasn't blushing, she could be even paler than usual, and she kept her voice and her hands steady. But if Rosalie hadn't come back with him she might have welcomed him with open invitation in her eyes and on her lips.

The sisters came fluttering into the room and Rosalie ran towards them. Mrs Fraser had told them she was here said Flora—she *was* the girl they wanted for Callum, thought Morag, she had to be. They acted as though she was their darling, kissing her, hugging her.

'What a lovely surprise,' said Dora. 'We knew Callum was meeting your father, but he never told us he was bringing you to see us.'

Morag had no part in this scene. Callum was drawn into it, all three women were smiling at him. Polly the Skye terrier frisked around Rosalie's feet, and Rosalie seated Flora in her chair, and leaned over the back of it, laughing, her long fair hair falling forwards. 'It was a surprise wasn't it?' she said gaily. 'But it's always like coming home here, and when Callum came to talk to Daddy, I asked him to bring me over, just for a night.'

'Dear child, we're always delighted to see you.' Dora patted Rosalie's cheek and Morag thought cynically—with her father in construction and Callum planning a hotel I could be seeing the start of a real marriage of convenience.

She felt as shut out as if they had pushed her into the hall and slammed the door. She knew that Callum was attracted to her, but their physical rapport would probably pass and Rosalie was ravishingly pretty and Callum's family adored her and for all Morag knew, he might too.

They all settled down, Rosalie sat on the footstool and Callum picked up the newspapers. 'You've met Morag of course,' Dora said after a while. 'Oh yes,' replied Rosalie and flashed a lovely smile then went on talking about people Morag had never heard of.

A Vanessa and a Jeremy were getting married and Rosalie was going to be a bridesmaid. She described the dress she would be wearing and the sisters hung on every word and Dora said Rosalie would be prettier than the bride. 'Say, how old is Vanessa?' Flora pondered.

'Eighteen,' said Rosalie.

'Of course, you were at school together. Eighteen is just the right age for a girl to get married, don't you think Callum?'

'For marrying Jeremy Purvis whose mental age is about fifteen it seems reasonable,' said Callum, and they all gave squeals of protest.

Dora scolded, 'Be serious now,' and when Morag left the room they hardly noticed.

She murmured, 'Will you excuse me?' and took herself off to the library. This was no business of hers, and it was something she probably wouldn't even bother to put into her letters. She had written a few in recent days to old friends and flatmates, telling them about the island and the castle, and the sisters and the others. But she had only mentioned Callum as the man who gave her the job and she probably wouldn't talk about Rosalie at all.

She had stationery and ballpoint pens in what had been an empty drawer under the long black-oak table that stood in the centre of the library. She sat down at the table now and took out a writing pad and wrote 'Calla Castle', the date, then 'Dear Jenny', and began to scribble away, but before she had written more than a few lines Callum walked in.

He wasn't looking for her of course, he was just going through to his office, but he grinned and she said, '*Very* pretty.'

'Always was,' he said. 'Right from the time she was a beautiful baby.'

'She's the chosen one is she?'

He reached her now, on the other side of the table. She sat, with her chin in her hand, and he stopped, looking at her across the expanse of dark oak. 'Whose choice?'

'Theirs obviously, yours maybe.' Her lips were curved and she went on mischievously, 'If her father's firm are building your hotel Rosalie could get you very good terms,' and he shook his head, laughing.

'What a mercenary woman you are. She's a nice child, but don't you think she's too young for me?'

'She'll get older.'

'So will I.'

You won't change that much, she thought. You're experienced and brilliant and tough. Nor will she change. She will always be like the sisters, enchanting as a kitten and no match for you under the skin. You can't marry her.

'I hope you'll be very happy,' she said, with only the faintest note of mockery and still smiling.

'I hope so too,' he said, 'I think we will.' And the smile died on her lips because he was not smiling and they were not talking of Rosalie. A nerve leapt in the softness of her throat, a flutter of panic, and for a few seconds they looked straight at each other. Then he said, 'I'll be in there for the rest of the evening.' In the office. 'And if you've got any sense you'll keep out of their way. They'll bore the pants off you.' He was grinning again as he moved and she called after him gaily, 'Don't be such a chauvinist.'

'It's too late to change the habits of a lifetime,' he said, closing the office door, and she picked up her pen again and went on with her letter.

He kept his word. He was working for the rest of the evening, or at any rate he kept away from the sisters and their guest. Morag went back after a while and sat with them in the drawing room and through the evening meal, and then back into the drawing room again.

Once Flora said it was too bad of Callum, not having any time to spare for them; but they were all used to it from the way they looked at each other, tolerant and understanding. 'His grandfather was never like this,' said Flora, 'but I don't know. Modern men! All they seem to think about is work.'

Rosalie was not one of the workers. At least not yet. She had left finishing school in Switzerland in the summer and now she was undecided what she was going to do. But she seemed to be having a pleasant enough time. She had just come back from a ski-ing holiday, and opportunities were opening for her.

Morag sat and listened as she discussed them. A friend who ran a boutique had offered her a partnership, and she had learned Cordon Bleu cooking and flower arranging and she might do a few dinner parties for friends. She had thought of taking a secretarial course because then Daddy might find a job for her in his offices.

'You're a very accomplished girl,' said Dora. 'And you'll make a wonderful wife.'

Rosalie smiled. 'That's what I'm trained for really isn't it?' And Morag felt sorry for her. If marriage was her ambition it should be no problem because she was beautiful and rich, but she was heading for heartache if she was hoping for Callum. And so were the match-making sisters. They were all living in a rosecoloured dream—anyone on the outside could see that Rosalie and Callum would be hopelessly ill-matched . . .

It was after midnight and Morag was reading when the knock came on her door. She had said goodnight to everybody and gone to her room the same time as the sisters. Callum had joined them by then and Rosalie was showing him some photographs that Flora had brought out of the bureau of Rosalie's holidays here as a child.

Morag was less tired than usual tonight. She was still working her way along the shelf of Victorian novels, and the cramped print needed concentration. The tap on the door made her jump. It was quick, secretive, and she thought—*Callum*! She hadn't expected him tonight. Some night yes, and soon, but this panicked her, so that she sat bolt upright, frozen.

She hadn't locked the door. After that once she hadn't bothered, and when the door began to open she gulped and Rosalie whispered, 'Are you awake?'

As the lights were on and Morag was sitting up, eyes wide open and holding a book, she was obviously awake, although Rosalie went on whispering, 'Can I talk to you?'

Morag's heart was still thumping. 'What about? she asked. 'What's the matter?'

Rosalie was wearing a white silk négligé that flowed demurely around her, and with her long pale hair she could have passed for a ghost, stealing barefoot along the corridors. 'Nothing,' said Rosalie. 'I just wanted to talk.' She drifted into the room now and sat on the side of the bed. 'I came to see you, you know. Lady

Ensor 'phoned my mother and said how attractive you were and that Callum had brought you here. You are attractive and I'm sure Callum thinks so. They're saying you're his . . .' She floundered, her face puckered like a child's.

Morag took pity on her and said, 'No.'

'His grandmother told me you came here because somebody broke your heart.'

'That's an exaggeration,' said Morag. 'Dented it maybe, and I needed a job and I thought I'd like to see Calla again and there was the job going with the sisters as companion-cum-secretary.'

'Calla? Not Callum? You're not in love with Callum?'

'I'm not in love with anyone.' That was the truth. It was not love. Within the limits of the flesh it was very much a force to be reckoned with, but it was not love.

'I adore him,' Rosalie said. Morag seemed to have reassured her that the field was clear. 'I always hoped he'd wait for me. Oh he's a special kind of man, he's so strong and so handsome and I just love the way he's always in charge. Nothing panics him. You know . . .'

She clasped her hands together, her face rapt and gleeful, and was into a tale of a runaway horse and how Callum had saved her. 'And he's a fabulous business man. My father says . . .'

She's back in the dorm, thought Morag. This is one of those after-lights-out all-girls-together chats with her schoolfriends. Callum is her hero, she probably sleeps with his picture under her pillow. When Rosalie stopped for breath Morag asked, 'How old *are* you?'

'Eighteen.'

'If I were you,' Morag said, 'I'd spread my wings. You're one of the prettiest girls I've ever seen. All sorts of marvellous men are going to be falling for you.'

'Do you really think so?' Rosalie's huge eyes glowed and she dimpled. 'Do you think Callum would be jealous? Wouldn't that be scary? I've never seen him angry but you get the feeling don't you . . .?' She shivered at the delicious thrill.

Morag said drily, 'I wouldn't recommend it. They do say he doesn't take after his grandfather.'

Rosalie giggled. She knew all about Flora's romances. 'I wouldn't want him to. He's one of the black Maconnells. One of the pirates. Have you noticed some of the old paintings?'

'Yes,' said Morag.

'I always hoped he'd wait for me, but I used to be scared he'd find somebody else before I grew up,' said Rosalie dreamily. 'Well of course he's found them, there've always been glamorous girls, but *really* found somebody I mean before I came down from finishing school and . . .' she gave her lovely ravishing smile, 'could really set out to get him.'

'Do you mean seduce him?' Morag almost squeaked.

Rosalie said, 'Don't you think I could?'

She had all the makings of a seductress, and Morag was sure that girls growing up with her had heard her say this and bolstered her confidence with their awe and envy. I'll bet you were the beauty queen of the finishing school, Morag thought.

Callum still considered Rosalie a child, but she was an adult in love and she had come here to size up Morag, who might have been a rival. She seemed reassured; or maybe this was a warning—lay off, he's mine; and in a contest Rosalie could be the winner.

Weariness was stealing over Morag. She yawned and said, 'I've enjoyed our little chat but I do need my sleep.'

'Of course,' said Rosalie. 'Good night.' At the door she turned to say as though it surprised her, 'I'm not a bit tired,' and then, 'I suppose that's because I'm so much younger than you.'

The kitten scratches, thought Morag, how old does she think I am? She nearly called before the door closed,

'Twenty-two last birthday, love,' but it wasn't worth rising to. She switched out the light and leaned back into the pillows and recognised the heaviness that had settled on her spirits as depression not weariness . . .

Rosalie and Callum left together next morning. Morag watched the helicopter rise and wished she could have gone with them. She had never felt imprisoned here before, but as it vanished into the clouds, free as a bird, she sighed.

The sisters hadn't come down. Rosalie had gone up to their room to say goodbye. Morag was in the kitchen, she had watched the helicopter through the window and Mrs Fraser was pouring tea for Maggie MacTavish who had just arrived to start her day's work.

'It's not raining this morning,' was Maggie's greeting as she took off her coat and sat down at the table.

'We had Miss Rosalie here for the night,' Mrs Fraser told her. 'Mr Callum brought her, they've just gone off together.'

'Is that a fact?' Maggie's little black eyes brightened. 'Still running round after him like a little puppy is she?'

'Growing into a real beauty,' said Mrs Fraser. 'Before long he's going to start noticing her.'

That seemed to please them both. 'She's always got what she wanted,' said Mrs Fraser. 'Right from when she was a baby.' She poured another cup of tea for Morag and continued, 'A bit spoilt of course but well, she's been reared to it hasn't she?'

The sisters were as bad. And as blinkered, Morag thought, because there was no way in which she would have said Rosalie was right for Callum. In Mrs Fraser's eyes she was a lady, because she had been reared in luxury and Mrs Fraser was all for the upper classes. And the sisters thought she was sweet and doting and pretty as a princess, and this morning they were singing her praises.

Morag always helped them deal with their mail but

that was soon done with and then Dora asked, 'What did you think of our Rosalie?'

'She's very pretty,' said Morag again.

'Oh she's a lovely girl,' said Flora. 'They'll be beautiful children won't they?' and Morag thought crazily, if they get her little face and Callum's big nose they could be striking but they won't be pretty. And she almost laughed, holding it down and tasting bitterness.

'Is it settled?' she asked, because for a moment she wondered what Rosalie might have told them when she said goodbye, and if Callum might have gone up with her.

'Not exactly,' said Flora and Morag let out a breath very softly. 'But I don't think it will be long.'

'Eighteen's young to get married,' Morag ventured.

'We got married at eighteen,' the sisters chorused, and Morag didn't point out that nearly sixty years ago there wasn't much else a woman could do.

For the first time Morag was reminded of the New Year's Eve Ball that was held at the castle. Rosalie's talk of the social whirl had probably made them think about Christmas festivities and themselves as glittering hostesses. It was the first week of November now and they suddenly said in chorus, 'Why don't we have our New Year's Eve party again?'

'We could be cut off by then,' Morag said, remembering when nothing could get in or out of the island, and Flora said that was defeatist talk and promptly dug out the last year's guest list while telling Morag that everyone had had a perfectly delightful time.

Mrs Fraser and Hamish took their instructions without a quiver as if they knew exactly what was expected of them. The same arrangements: rooms prepared for overnight guests, the food, the drink, the pipers, the fiddlers. Morag sat silently by, and hoped they weren't all going to be disappointed with all the trouble being for nothing.

Callum came back again that night and she told him, 'They're organising a New Year's Eve party. I suppose it's a tradition, but what happens if we get cut off and nobody can get here? The last Christmas I was on Calla I remember . . .'

'That was the last time it happened so early,' he said. 'We're usually accessible until January or February. I thought they might let it go this year but I suppose Rosalie was chattering about it.'

Morag hadn't heard her but she might have done, and he said, 'Let them have their party,' as though he was humouring children . . .

By the end of November it was cold with a bone-stripping intensity for which Morag's years in the south had left her unprepared. Great fires were kept burning and the central heating was turned up but she muffled herself in thick clothes and thick tights and, when she ventured outside, stuffed her hair into a woolly hat, wrapped a scarf around her neck and wore boots and two pairs of gloves.

But she was getting used to being here. The routine of her life was suiting her. She was always on hand for the sisters. They said she was a treasure, and perhaps she spoiled them too because she was very fond of them.

The memoirs were coming on. She typed page after page from the notes she took while they trotted out anecdotes from their lives with a mass of details. Morag found it fascinating. She went on cataloguing the library, she helped Mrs Fraser, she busied herself, and Callum came back again and again.

She never missed the sound of the helicopter now. Wherever she was she heard it and sometimes it seemed to her that all her life she had been here, holding her breath until it touched down safely.

They talked easily, lightly, but the magnetism between them was strong and she knew that the end was inevitable. One day or night they would become lovers, she hoped it would not be an end but a beginning but she had no way of being sure. She dreamed of him, she longed for him, but the first move must come from Callum because that would give her a slight edge of control. She was not offering, she would let him tell her that he wanted her and not just with a look but say it, ask, so that there was no doubt at all.

Each Friday she 'phoned Alistair, although there was not much to report, except that she had settled in. She had told him about the plans for the hotel, but they were just plans until next year. Nothing would be happening until the spring. No other visitors had come, the sisters organised the New Year's Ball and kept in touch with their friends by 'phone and mail. Although a couple of times Callum brought business colleagues back with him.

The second one was a middle-aged Canadian, grey haired, grey suited, good company over dinner and charming to the ladies but obviously astute. After dinner he and Callum went into the office and that was the last Morag saw of either, unless you counted the helicopter rising next morning.

She told Alistair about him in her Friday evening call. Alistair never told her much except that he was fine, and sometimes she found it hard to make any contact at all.

Her brother seemed so far away. The ferry was still running once a week now, the helicopter was coming and going, but when she was talking to Alistair the castle and the island seemed as if they were on another planet.

He was still bitter about Callum, whom he never referred to by name. 'Is he there?' he'd ask and Morag would say yes or no, and that was usually all. She volunteered no information, there was never anything to say, and Alistair would rant a little. But when she said, 'We had one visitor this week. A business man, rather a sweetie,' Alistair asked, 'What was his business?'

'I don't know. They were in the office all evening.'

'This office,' said Alistair. 'Have you ever been in it?'

'Once.' That first night, when she was carried in.

'I'd like to be a fly on the wall in there,' said Alistair. He went on, quickly, quietly, 'If you kept your eyes and your ears open you might learn a few things that could be useful.'

'About what?' she began, but he didn't wait. 'I've been thinking, you've got a chance to wise yourself up on what he's up to. Does he keep files in that office? Is there anything about this place because there's a rumour going round that he might be selling?'

'I'll ask him if you like,' she offered.

'I wouldn't believe a word he says,' said Alistair. 'But if you could find a file.'

'They're computers.' She remembered that. 'I'd look a right idiot mucking about with them.' And then the emormity of it struck her and she said, 'I'll ask him but I'm not spying for you.'

'You think that would be a dirty trick do you?' said Alistair. 'Then you're an idiot. The way he's treated you, keeping you walled up on Calla, I should think you'd be glad of the chance to make your stay worth while.'

Industrial espionage! Crack the code, listen at doors and learn the secrets of the Maconnell empire. It wasn't meant as a joke but it was, a lousy one. She said, 'You must be out of your mind. I'm not going to be found going through his papers or with my fingers on his computer.'

'You like him don't you?' said Alistair accusingly.

'Yes,' said Morag. 'I like them all. Even Mrs Fraser on a good day. *And* I can tell Hyde from Jekyll now.'

'God almighty!' Alistair exploded and she put down the 'phone.

December brought in the storms. The grey skies were broken by black clouds rolling in from the Atlantic, winds began lashing the waves so that they crashed against the cliffs and broke over the landing stage and the harbour wall.

Small storms as yet but they made Morag uneasy. There was the helicopter hopping in and out and the sisters worried about that and so did Morag. She sat there, as tense as either of them, every night they were expecting Callum back. When he was out of Scotland for a while it was almost a relief although she missed him.

She wondered what he was doing and who he was with. Nobody told her, nobody here knew. Out there was where the money was made that paid for the upkeep of the castle, the sisters knew that but they had no interest in the nitty-gritty of trade and commerce. Morag wished they had, she would have liked to hear and not—emphatically not—to pass on to Alistair.

They hoped he was seeing Rosalie. They thought that likely and talked about it happily, and Morag listened to distant thunder and broke out in a cold sweat. Storms had not bothered her for years but here it was different, because it was here that the storm had taken her father's boat and the three men aboard and washed one man up a week later with a few pieces of driftwood. The other man, and her father, the sea had kept. Now she was back on Calla she remembered that storm and the night of waiting and it didn't seem so long ago.

When Callum came back almost the first thing his grandmother asked him was, 'Did you see Rosalie?'

'No,' he said. 'Why?'

'Well,' she was a little put-out, 'you've been gone for nearly two weeks, we thought that surely . . . What *have* you been doing?'

'Earning a living,' he said, and grinned at Morag.

'Did you get down to the Midlands by any chance? Did you see my brother?' she asked him.

'No to both,' said Callum, 'but I hear he's all right. Don't you?'

'Oh we talk on the 'phone,' she said. Only they hadn't for the last fortnight, it would be three weeks if she didn't call him tonight. She had offended Alistair and saying she liked Callum had been the last straw, but she was still sore at his suggestion that she should sneak into the office and snoop around. She asked outright, 'He said he's heard a rumour that you might be selling the centre.'

'If he has,' said Callum, 'that's all it is. A rumour.'

It was an answer of sorts, and she had to be satisfied with it because it was all she was getting. 'There's another storm coming up,' said Flora. 'A bad one, I'm starting to get a headache. I wish you wouldn't fly when the weather's like this.'

Morag had been thinking that Callum was coming and so was the storm, most of the day. The winds had dropped an hour ago and the sea looked like pewter, almost still but it was a sinister silence. The sky was black and purple and Morag knew that the worst storm yet would break over the island before long.

She would 'phone Alistair. It didn't look as if he was going to ring her but he was still her brother and she worried about him and at their usual time she dialled his number. He answered almost as soon as it rang. 'Hello,' she said.

'I was just going to call you.'

'Great minds,' she smiled. 'You wouldn't be having a storm down there too?'

'Storm?' said Alistair. 'No. It's trying to snow though.' The line was crackling and she raised her voice and they both almost shouted at the same time, 'How are you?'

'All right,' she said. 'Callum says it is only a rumour about him selling the centre.'

'You believe that? You're still getting on all right with him?' Alistair sounded as if he was choosing his words carefully, and when she said she was he went on, 'I've been doing some thinking. If you can't get any inside business tips you could at least ask him to let up. I mean I'm paying him back every month but if he'd take less and wait longer it would be less of a bloody treadmill. And if the two of you are on—well good terms, it shouldn't be much to ask.'

Static punctuated his words, and when he stopped and what sounded like a burst of firecrackers took over she said reluctantly, 'I suppose I could try, but I can't promise and don't bank on anything.'

It was an appalling line. They gave up after another couple of minutes and she put down the 'phone. She usually used the one in the hall, which was set into an alcove and as private as any. She sat there for a little while, wondering if she *could* ask Callum to change the terms of their arrangement.

She did get on 'all right' with him. He fancied her—probably less than she fancied him did he but know it, but how would he react to her wheedling on behalf of her light-fingered brother? He might think she was bargaining with her sex appeal. Alistair did. Alistair thought they were lovers. It had riled him for three weeks and then he had started wondering how it could be used to his advantage.

She didn't see how she could make out a case why her brother should not pay what he owed without seeming to be putting herself up as part payment and that was unthinkable. She could hear the wind rising now, a high eldritch keening like some unearthly chorus. Here comes the storm she thought, as she went back to the others.

The sisters had sleeping pills, for emergencies. 'If this is going on all night we'll be needing our pills,' said Flora over dinner, because by then the storm was raging overhead, and Morag could have done with a few pills herself.

It wasn't so bad while everyone was up. The castle had its own generator so the lights burned steadily, and with windows fastened and heavy curtains drawn the storm was almost locked out, but she hoped she was not going to lie listening to it. She hoped she would be able to pull the bedclothes over her head and think about something else.

The pills were only taken when they were under stress, and when their bedtime came round Morag tipped out a pill each from the little bottle and waited until they had swallowed.

She always came up with them now. Sometimes she helped them into bed although usually they said good night as soon as they were unhooked and unzipped. Tonight they kept her for a while before they decided they could manage from then on and she went along to her own room.

She wondered if Alistair was still using sleeping pills, remembering the horror of that morning when she had thought he'd taken an overdose. He could have done, and he still could if he got utterly down and depressed again. Then she really would be alone.

The curtains were open in her room and the night sky was an eerie shade of green. The winds were gale force and the rain was crashing against the window like the waves of the sea. She stood holding the curtain, knowing that a blanket over her head would not keep her from remembering that it was in a storm like this that her father's boat had foundered and he had drowned, and she began shivering as though the freezing water was covering her too and backed away from the window. She did not want to be alone. Callum would be downstairs. They had left him in the drawing room. She would go down and ask for a drink, and maybe she could tell him she was worried about Alistair, because that was reasonable, he would surely understand that.

She hurried along the corridor, almost running, because she was suddenly sure he would be waiting for her and that only in his arms would she get safely through the night . . . .

CHAPTER FIVE

Lights were still burning. Hamish always went round turning them off before he turned in, but they were burning in the hall and in the little drawing room. Only the room was empty, there wasn't even a dog.

Callum could be anywhere. He might be with the Frasers, he might be in his office. She went to the library first, hearing the storm above the sound of her own footsteps, seeing the green light of it through the long mullioned windows so that it was like being at the bottom of the sea, and tapped on the office door and got no reply. But the door was heavy oak and perhaps he had answered and she couldn't hear him. She didn't know if this door was kept locked, she had never tried to open it before, but now she lifted the weighty latch and looked inside.

'Hello,' she said.

Lights were on in here too. Wall lights and the desk light so he couldn't be far away, but this room was empty except for Jekyll who got up as she walked in. 'Where's your master?' she asked inanely.

Callum wouldn't have left the office lights on and gone to bed, he must be coming back here, and she stepped in and looked around. There *was* a filing cabinet, although she wouldn't have opened that for a fortune, and presumably he did his own typing and filing, unusual in a man in his position. Maybe I could help, she thought. He'd provided a typewriter for the memoirs, she could do some typing for him maybe.

Another dog came padding up alongside her, although the door into the library was shut, and she whirled around and Callum was there. The wall panelling in the office concealed another door. She jumped a good inch then sagged, gasping, 'I was waiting for you but I didn't expect you to come out of the wall.'

'Were you?' he enquired. 'Why?'

He hadn't been waiting for her. It had been a crazy idea that all she had to do was come down and she wouldn't have to give any explanation. She said, 'I thought you might like company for another hour or so because I would. It's the storm.'

'Do storms bother you?' She hadn't shown any fear earlier tonight, and it wasn't fear so much as the lonely memories.

'I didn't think so,' she admitted, 'but this is a humdinger.'

'They often are in the winter. Had you forgotten?'

'In the summer too, sometimes,' she said. 'One came up like this when my father's boat was out. We couldn't stand outside for the wind. We waited all night, the cottage was full of women waiting with us. But he never came back. And we left Calla as soon as Willie Muir was washed up.'

Sometime while she was speaking he had crossed the little space between them and put his arms around her. 'It'll be all right after this one,' she said. 'It's the first bad storm.' She felt safe and comforted, with a rising hunger for more that was soon going to be uncontrollable.

She had dreamed of herself in Callum's arms night after night, but suddenly she was scared because once she let go here she would be out of her depth and out of her mind and with no way of knowing what might happen to her.

She turned towards the open door and said, 'I never knew there was another room in there.'

His arm was still around her, but he made no move to hold her tighter. 'Not much more than a cupboard,' he said. 'But it takes a single bed.'

She felt her cheeks burning and thought he was going to start laughing, and when she made herself look him in the face there was more than a glint of amusement in his eyes. 'That's handy,' she said. 'You can sleep near your work. Talking of work couldn't you use a secretary? Do you do your own typing and filing? Somehow I shouldn't have thought you could type.'

That was a loony thing to say. Her voice died and the sound of the wind took over, and she thought—I'm whistling in the dark. I want him and he knows it and yet I couldn't be more nervous if I was being backed into an alley by a mugger.

She could hardly run for it after she had come down and said she needed company through the storm. Not while the storm was still raging, and anyhow she didn't want to run. She just wanted her teeth to stop chattering so that she could start acting her age. She thought—I bet Rosalie wouldn't be moving away and sitting in the middle of the sofa, and making banal conversation. 'Would it be a cheek to ask for a drink?'

He brought a brandy bottle and two glasses, and looked at her with concern and asked, 'All right?' as if he thought it was the storm and memories that were making her tense and strained.

She nodded and smiled a tight little smile. At least the night was young, she had time to pull herself together. She swallowed some brandy and wondered at herself because this was ridiculous. She didn't even know she had inhibitions and now, with the first man she had ever wanted so that she felt she might starve to death without him, she needed a stiff drink before she could give anything at all.

He sat in the captain's chair, his glass on the desk in front of him. There wasn't room to join her on the sofa while she kept to the middle of it, and she gulped down a little more and remembered Alistair knocking it back and sighed and Callum said, 'Trouble? Apart from the storm?'

If she talked about Alistair she would have to be rational and calm. 'My brother,' she said. 'I'm beginning to think his middle name's trouble. He's finding the payments tough.'

'He's meant to,' said Callum drily.

'Only I was wondering, I suppose you wouldn't change the terms and make it easier on him?'

'No.'

'Well it was worth a try.' She turned her glass round and round in her hands. 'Only when I was giving them the sleeping pills just now I remembered he takes them, and I thought about that morning you came . . .'

'I think he's too selfish to be a suicide risk,' Callum said. But Alistair was weak, although she had never realised it, and Callum could not understand weakness and she said bitterly,

'He's not your brother. You don't care.'

'You do?' She couldn't tell what he was thinking. She rarely could, except for those flashes of sexual awareness that passed between them. But perhaps if he knew how much Alistair meant to her it might influence him and she said warmly, 'Of *course* I do, I'd do anything for him,' and was taken aback when the hard lines of his face dissolved into a grin.

'We do have trouble with our relations don't we?' he said.

In recent months she had all right, and he sounded like a fellow sufferer. 'Do you?' she asked.

'Do you need to ask? The Flora-Dora twins! It's like having two spoiled children on your hands.' If he married Rosalie he would have another but she knew what he meant. 'This New Year's Eve Ball now,' Callum went on. 'If we are in for a grim winter it could be you and me, the Frasers, Flora and Dora and anyone who can stagger up the hill.'

'Don't say I didn't warn you,' she said gaily.

'I won't if you don't remind me.'

'Dora's been a widow a long time hasn't she?'

'Since Great-uncle Hugo tried to take a horse over a hedge that was too high. The horse had more sense than he had, it stopped. He'd already lost a fortune to the bookies—never backed a winner in his life they said—and that proved it, he should have left horses alone.'

'It surely did,' she said. 'Poor Dora.'

'Poor Dora's quite enjoyed fifty years as a widow.'

'But it's Flora who's got the letters.'

'That isn't to say that Dora's score wasn't as high.'

She gurgled, 'Ach, you're a terrible cynic.'

'Not particularly, I'm telling you about my family.'

'The old laird was lovely.' Not that Morag had seen much of him, she didn't think she had ever spoken to him, but everyone had said he was a grand old man and he had been easy to work for. Too easy, as Alistair had found when the reckoning came.

'One of the best,' Callum agreed. 'Heart of gold. And daft as a brush in business matters. I was in Canada most of the time, we're solvent there. But when I took over the lot I got a shock.'

This sip of brandy made her cough. 'Had a—lot of people swindled him?'

'They had.'

'I'm sorry.' It was no excuse that Alistair was one of many.

Callum shrugged. 'It must have been like taking candy from a baby. Hard to resist if you're that way inclined.'

Nobody would cheat Callum, the hard man who played to win and to hold, and she wondered aloud, 'How often does a Maconnell like you turn up to restore the family fortunes?'

'Funny you should say that. That is how it seems to happen. How often does one like you turn up?'

She wasn't tense any more. His gaze took her in slowly from head to toe and he was smiling and she smiled too because he so obviously approved of what he saw.

'Fairly regularly I should think, only there are no paintings to prove it.' She made a small grimace. 'I'm fairly run of the mill,' and she knew he would deny it.

'Oh no, Morag Macdonald, you're a rare bird.'

There was something special about her tonight, a touch of magic, and it wasn't the brandy that was giving her the inner glow. It was him making her smile until she was smiling at herself and she knew that it had been stupid to be afraid. After that moment of panic she had no reservations at all. It was as though they had known each other all their lives and would never be apart again.

'When you build your hotel will you find me a job?' she asked, and knew he would refuse her nothing, and just as surely she could never refuse him.

'Of course, if you want to stay on Calla.' His dark eyes held hers and his voice was smiling.

'It's home,' she said. 'What shall I do?'

'How about showing the public around the castle?'

That made her sit up. If tourists came to Calla letting them into the castle would be another attraction. 'Shall you open it? Do they know?'

The sisters knew about the hotel but they had said nothing about any plans for their home, and she wasn't surprised when he said, 'I haven't discussed it with them. Anyhow I thought we might start with the north wing, so they'd hardly notice.'

That had been shut off as long as Morag remembered, and she asked, 'How long is it since it was used?'

'The rooms were emptied about the turn of the century. The doors were locked about thirty years ago.'

'And nobody's been in there since?'

'I don't think so. Except for me. I used to wander around in there as a boy.' He grinned, a lop-sided grin. 'I still do sometimes.'

'On your own?'

'That is the idea.'

She liked him telling her what she was almost sure he had told no one else and she joked, 'If you'd let me have a key I needn't go out in the rain and get my hair frizzed.'

'I like your hair frizzed, and you wouldn't have been safe on your own.'

This time he was concerned about her, not about the trouble she would cause if she had an accident. Although maybe he had been the last time too, when he had ordered her to keep out. 'I was going to find the key someday,' she confessed. 'I wasn't leaving here without exploring the north wing.'

'I'll take you round.'

'When?'

'Tomorrow.'

Lord knows why she said, 'It's tomorrow now,' except that she was bubbling with gaiety as though she had drunk a large bottle of champagne instead of a small brandy.

'I'll get you a coat,' he said, 'it will be cold,' and she was left open-mouthed. She hadn't expected to go exploring in the middle of the night. She had thought they would wait for daylight. Of course they wouldn't be roaming around but it would be quite a thrill to see a door swing open and peer where no one had gone for thirty years. Except Callum. The night of the storm was turning into an adventure and a lark, and when he came back, carrying a dark fur coat and a torch she said, 'You're mad, and whose is that?'

'I got it out of a cupboard in their dressing room.' There was a rail of furs in the wardrobes although Morag couldn't remember either of the sisters wearing this particular one. It looked like sable. It must belong to one of them. She said, 'I suppose you didn't ask if I might borrow it?'

'I opened the door and they were both snoring beautifully.'

'Well,' she said, 'I hope they wouldn't mind. I do have a coat of my own you know.' But he held this coat for her and she slipped her arms into it and was enveloped in luxury. She had never in her life worn a coat like this before, not even on her few modelling jobs. It must have been full length on the sisters, it came to mid-calf on Morag and with the collar turned up she felt like one of those fairy-tale princesses, who travelled in horse-drawn sleighs over the icy wastes.

He was wearing a dark overcoat, he held out his hand to her and she took it. As their fingers locked she thought, I'd go out into the icy wastes with you, with my hand in yours I'd leap into darkness; and that was exactly what she seemed to be doing.

The touch of their hands was like a commitment although neither spoke, and as they walked together, across the hall towards the corridor that ended in a door that led into the north wing, they began joking again. She asked, 'Is it dusty in there? I'd hate to get cobwebs on this coat.'

He smiled and said, 'I'll brush you down before we put it back.'

The key turned smoothly in the lock and the door opened silently. She would have expected the lock to be stiff and the door to creak, but if Callum was opening the wing to the public he had probably been in here recently. 'No electricity,' he said, and shone the powerful beam of the torch down the corridor.

All the castle was old. Seven hundred years at least, they said. But the living quarters had the luxury of papered and panelled walls, carpets and paintings and beautiful furninture. The ruggedness there was civilised. Here the walls and the floors were rock grey and icy air surged out so that she wrapped the coat closer around her.

Callum had loosed her hand and she stood alone and he asked 'Do you want to go in?'

There were no windows in this passage. It was like peering into a long cavern where the beam of the torch only gave limited lighting. A leap in the dark, she thought. 'Of course,' she replied and walked in with him and was startled when he closed the door into the hall behind them.

'The dogs aren't used to it,' he explained, 'and there are unsafe parts.'

'That makes sense.' She shivered. 'Only I hope you can find this door again.'

'Trust me. When they locked the doors I was away at boarding school, just turned seven years old. I found a key and kept it and nobody ever missed it. So the north wing was mine.'

A room of their own was the height of most kids' ambitions, with a treehouse or a garden shed if they were lucky, but all this ... 'No wonder you grew up with delusions of grandeur,' she said. 'A whole wing of a castle for your secret pad.'

Some doors were open, through the windows of rooms beyond the storm was still lighting up the sky. There had probably been gaslight in here but it was easier to imagine the walls carrying flaming torches and great candelabras of candles burning. Everywhere was empty and echoing and that made it seem awesomely vast. You could have built a row of cottages in some of those rooms.

'Did you ever have a secret pad?' he asked her.

'I'll tell you something,' her arm was linked in his and they went so easily and comfortably together, 'when I did need to get away I used to escape by daydreaming that I was up here in the castle. I came up a few times with my mother. Not often. Only as a very occasional treat, and then I could wander around so long as I didn't touch—and I really didn't except the odd library book and those blessed pearls ...'

They smiled at each other and her heart stilled and he bent his head and kissed her and the sweetness of it pierced her. Then something scuttled just ahead and she shot up in his arms. 'We do have squatters,' he said. She could see great festoons of spiders' webs now that her eyes were used to the dark, and that had been either a mouse or a rat. There were probably bats too. But the kiss was still tingling in her blood so that even snakes would hardly have daunted her.

'They've got rights by now,' she said. 'You won't be able to just evict them you know,' and they went on into a maze of passages until she stopped to ask, 'Where does that lead to?'

They were at an archway from which a flight of steps curved, and he said, 'You're unbelievable. That is the tower.'

'So why does it make me unbelievable?'

'I'll show you.'

The steps, cut in the rock, went dizzily up and round, with an occasional cross-slit window on the way. The walls were running damp, there was no handrail and the steps were slippery. He followed close behind her, hand steadying her, the torch lighting her, he seemed surefooted and she climbed slowly and carefully right to the top.

Then she knew what he meant, because this had to be the room he had come to over the years. In a very spartan fashion this was furnished. There was a camp bed but no bedding, a wooden kitchen chair and a small plain table. 'Stylish,' she said.

'Glad you like it.' He led her towards the window. 'There's not likely to be anyone out there tonight or there might have been tales of a light in the north wing and the ghost of Mad Maconnell.'

'Was there a Mad Maconnell?'

He laughed, his arm around her waist, her head on his shoulder. 'If you ask me, fifty per cent of them could qualify. I needed this place to get away from my relations and their friends. From here on a clear day you can see for ever.'

Rising so high on the very edge of the cliffs there was a commanding view over the open sea. Nothing could approach Calla on this side of the island without being spotted from this tower if a watcher stood here. Which must have been handy in the days of clan warfare or when the Vikings came raping and pillaging in their long ships.

'On a dark night,' she said, 'it's still a fearsome sight.'

The storm was playing itself out but lightning was still silvering the blackness of sky and sea. You could still hear the thunder rolling and the waves crashing, and she stood, cradled against the dark man, and she could feel his heartbeats like her own.

'You're not scared by the storm now?' he said.

'I'm not scared,' she replied but they were not talking about the storm, and it was as though all her life so far had been bringing her to this time at this place.

'Good,' he said. His hands were on her shoulders, under the soft fur of the coat, pulling her up tight against him, and she raised her face, offering her parted lips. At the touch of his mouth her bones melted, the only strength in her was to cling to him, all her senses singing at the taste of his tongue. The rising tide of sensation from the deep possession of that kiss spread through her until she was digging her fingers into the back of his neck, straining against him, slipping down in his arms.

She was mindless now. Some wild spirit had taken her over, and a fire in her blood was out of control. Under his skilled caressing hands she was flaming and soaring, as though he knew every nerve in every inch of her, just as she knew and gloried in the lovely magical territory of his body.

It seemed incredible that there could be such searing

joy without burning up like a meteorite, but while she was begging, 'No more'—only the words wouldn't come—there always was. She was insatiable, never wanting it to stop, and then the castle shook, and the earth shook, and if it was the thunder that was fitting because they were both up there on the crest of the storm; and she was floating and sobbing and utterly completely exhausted and content.

She might have slept a little while. Or maybe she just lay in a warm drowsy dream, but when she opened her eyes he was sitting beside her. She could see in the dark like a cat. She could see his face so clearly, and the way he was looking down at her, and she thought she had never opened her eyes before and been so happy to wake.

'Would you believe I didn't plan that?' he said. 'Not here. Next time we'll find a softer couch.' He brushed her hair back from her face and his touch was gentle.

'Would you believe I thought we had?' The floor should have been hard but she wouldn't have noticed anyway and she started tugging her clothing into order and he kissed her bare shoulder as she pulled on her sweater and said huskily, 'You are incredibly beautiful.'

'Mmm.' She felt incredible. 'Oh my gosh,' she said. 'The coat. Is the coat all right?'

He smiled. 'It's all right and I can always tell them I gave it to you.'

'No, you cannot.' She stood up and shook the coat out and said, 'It's bound to be dusty. It could have got ripped to shreds, at the very least.'

'Madam, what kind of an animal do you take me for?'

She laughed. 'Well this is a lucky coat.' The icy atmosphere was getting to her again, she slipped her arms back into the sleeves, found her shoes and put those on again, and took a step and kicked the torch spinning it against the stone wall.

She must have slept for a few minutes, because Callum was not dishevelled at all. He was dressed for walking, he must have had a little time while Morag lay, cocooned in sable, out for the count. She was still not quite steady, slightly lightheaded. She thought, my goodness I shall sleep tonight, and yawned. Then she heard the click of the torch, which he had picked up, and no light came and her yawn sagged into a gasp, 'Is it broken?'

He unscrewed the torch and reported, 'The bulb's smashed.'

'Oh, how clumsy of me.'

She could see him all right, and the room, but of course she couldn't see like a cat, it was all dim and shadowy; and now the lightning had finished flashing and there was no moon nor stars, just blackness outside the castle and in. And although Callum knew his way around in here that didn't mean he would remember every inch of rotting wood and fallen masonry.

'Do you have any matches?' she asked.

'No.'

'What are we going to do?'

'We could wait for the dawn.'

Dawn broke late on Calla this time of year and although she wouldn't mind at all passing the rest of the night together she would prefer them to be out of the north wing, where it was icy cold and things were scuttling and flying. 'Or I could get you out,' he said.

'Without a light?'

'I don't usually come in here in the dark but I do know where we should be putting our feet.'

She was sure he did. He was smiling at her, and she would go with him anywhere. She gave a little chuckle of relief. 'Then let's go.'

'When I deliver you safely to your bedroom may I come in?'

She took his hand and said, 'Don't let me fall off the

edge of anything and all right.' At the door she turned to look back and ask, 'What shall you tell them about this room when you throw it open to the public?'

'After tonight,' he said, 'nobody else gets in here.' And he lifted her fingers to his lips.

It was so dark that sometimes they seemed to be walking through deep mines, and it seemed much farther because they were slower. There were noises too, from the squatters. Squeaks and scuttlings that their voices had drowned before. But now they didn't talk so much, concentrating on their route, and when Callum said, 'Here we are,' another few steps brought them to the door.

'Honestly I never doubted you for a moment. I just thought we were going the pretty way round,' she said with a laugh.

Jekyll and Hyde were still in the hall, and they watched Callum and Morag get in the lift, with what she could have sworn was disapproval. It was good to be back where there was comfort and comparative warmth, and as they walked along the corridor towards her room, fatigue made her footsteps drag. She was so very tired, she was drained emotionally and physically. All she was fit for was falling into bed and falling asleep, and when they reached her room she looked up at Callum with heavy-lidded eyes she could hardly keep open. 'Good night. I know what I said but,' he could see she was worn out and she raised her shoulders in an exaggerated shrug, 'so I cheat,' she said.

'Do you now?' he said, and she thought sleepily— that was the wrong word, I shouldn't have said that, it has bad connections. But he kissed her cheek, as gently as though he was kissing a child. 'Sleep well.'

She almost wished he wouldn't go, that he would come into the room with her and lie by her, letting her fall asleep in the crook of his arm. But he went down the corridor without looking back. She went into her room, shedding her clothes in a pile on the floor, and crawled into bed. She tried to lie awake long enough to savour the past hour or two, because it had been out of this world. But her cheek had hardly touched the pillow before she was deep asleep.

When she woke, almost before she opened her eyes, she began to smile. What had happened last night had been more than making love. That had been inevitable. She hadn't realised how wonderful it would be but she had always known they were on a sexual collision course. But what he had told her about the north wing had almost meant more than sex because she knew there had been other women but she didn't believe he had ever taken anyone else into the room in the tower. He was a man who kept his defences high but she had the key, and this morning she felt that there was nothing now they could not share, nothing she need hide from him.

She hoped they would go on as lovers, and for a while at least they surely would, but she was sure this morning that they could always be friends.

She put the coat back in the dressing room on her way downstairs to collect the sisters' breakfast tray. In the kitchen Hamish and Mrs Fraser and Maggie were talking about the storm and Hamish was glumly predicting a bad winter. Upstairs again the sisters were quieter than usual. Sleeping pills had given them an undisturbed night but they were both sluggish this morning and Morag left them still in their beds, silently sipping their hot water and lemon.

The 'phone rang in the alcove as she crossed the hall, she picked up the receiver and said, 'Calla Castle.' Jeckyll was stretched out on a rug, still looking reproachfully at her she could swear—which had to be her guilty conscience, and she pulled a face at the dog as she answered the 'phone.

'Morag?' Alistair's voice came through the earpiece.

'Oh it's you. Yes it's me. This is a bit early isn't it? I'm surprised the 'phones are still working after last night's storm. Is anything the matter?'

'No more than yesterday. How did you get on?'

'With what?'

'With him of course. You have got to him haven't you? You have softened him up? So is he going to go easy on these repayments? You did ask him didn't you?'

'I did,' she said, 'but——' and then Callum's voice took over.

'She did, and it was a pleasant try, but you overestimate her powers of persuasion.' He sounded amused, the 'phone clicked as his receiver was replaced, and there was silence until Alistair's horrified croak, 'Was that him?'

'Who else would it be?' If she hadn't put down the 'phone herself she would have screamed at him, but then she almost burst into tears, which would have been just as useless. She had to talk to Callum. She had to explain. He knew she was worried about Alistair, that was almost the first thing they had discussed last night, but he could never believe what happened afterwards had any bearing on that.

So where was he? She was desperately calm, forcing herself to think not panic. He must have picked up the receiver at the same time she did so he was near a 'phone. Down here there were extensions in the small drawing room and in his office. She went to the library, walking fast because if she hesitated she could decide she couldn't face him yet. And she had to face him and explain it wasn't how it sounded.

She knocked on the door and she heard him say, 'Come in,' and she thought he was waiting for her because although he had papers on his desk he was sitting back in his chair. He smiled but it was not all right, and she said, 'You knew he was finding the payments hard going, I told you that.'

'And that you'd do anything for him.'

'There are limits, for heaven's sake,' she shrilled.

'No matter.' As if it really didn't matter, and not for the right reasons but as if it wasn't worth bothering about. 'But one point we should clear up,' he said. 'Your brother seemed to know what was likely to happen last night, and I'm sure most of the men you meet probably are lusting after you so why should I be the exception? But where he is on the wrong track is this "You have got to him" business.' He shook his head, looking as cynical and as handsome as the devil. 'You're very desirable, I enjoyed having you, but I should stress that except in a purely physical sense, you would be unlikely to get to me in a hundred years. So long as that's understood I'm at your service anytime.'

She spat out a mouthful of fishwife Gaelic that she had forgotten she knew, and he threw back his head and laughed at her. 'Don't let anyone ever try to turn you into a lady, Morag Macdonald.'

She hated his arrogance. Every blessed thing about him she hated. 'It would be as hopeless as passing you off as a gentleman,' she replied waspishly.

'And yet both our fathers were gentlemen.'

She hadn't known he knew anything about her father, who had been kind and honourable, a good man, a gentleman. She wanted to say, 'If you hadn't picked up the telephone you wouldn't be talking like this because it wasn't like that. So why can't we pretend you didn't hear.' But if he could believe that she had calculated and contrived last night she would be wasting her breath.

I am getting away from Calla, she thought, by the first ferry, the first boat. She was through being hostage for Alistair. From now on her brother was on his own.

'Don't you ever lay a finger on me again,' she said 'or I'll scream rape.' She tried to slam the door behind her as she walked out, but it was too heavy and she only managed a small thud.

She went back to her room to start packing but when she heard the helicopter she was pacing the carpet because her hands were shaking too badly to do anything. She watched it, standing back from the window, arms folded, hands gripping. I hope you go down in the sea, she thought. I hope you dive five fathoms deep. And she remembered her father and countless others and thought, I am sick, how could I wish that on anyone. And black depression overwhelmed her so that she stumbled into her little bathroom and stood over the bowl, sobbing great tearless sobs that shook her with retching.

At least Callum was out of the castle. They hadn't expected him to leave this morning so that had been a recent decision and it could have been because he was as anxious to put space between them as she was. Or it could have nothing at all to do with her. It could be business and he could be back again tonight.

But he had gone now and she might be gone by tonight. 'Pack,' she ordered herself, staring at her white face in the mirror over the handbasin. She felt as hollow and shaky as if she had had a long illness that had knocked all the guts out of her. Packing wouldn't take long. She could throw her things into her case within minutes. First she would go down and tell the Frasers she had had this 'phone call and she had to leave and ask how she could get away.

She had friends whose homes were on open invitation to her, and when she reached the mainland she would make for a small hotel, stay overnight and do some 'phoning. Her bank account was peanuts but it would tide her over. All she needed was a roof for a few days while she got herself together. Which she would. She always did. But now the effort the upheaval was going to entail seemed almost too much.

She made her bed and tidied her room. I have to go, I have to go, she was telling herself all the time, and perhaps she should tell the sisters first. They were beginning to rely on her, and although nobody could keep her here—and Callum was not likely to try—she did owe them that courtesy.

She heard them talking as she came down the stairs into the hall. She must have been longer in her room than she had realised. Their voices floated through the open door of the small drawing room and when she walked in they both told her, 'Callum's gone.'

'I heard the helicoper,' she said.

'We thought he was staying for the weekend at least,' said Flora dolefully, 'but he's left a note saying he's off to Brussels.'

He wouldn't be back from there tonight which meant that Morag had a little more time to beat a dignified retreat. 'Nice for Brussels,' she muttered.

Dora said, 'The mail got through, there are two letters for you.' Morag took the two envelopes Dora was offering her. One was from a young farmer's wife in Wiltshire and she thought wryly—I wonder if Gail and Robert would have me for Christmas. She didn't recognise the other writing so she sat down and opened that envelope first.

It was crazy that she didn't know Kevin's hand. She would have recognised his paintings anywhere but during the six months or so of their affair they had never needed to write to each other. He had always lived three miles up the road and they had gone from date to date, 'phoning if there was any change in plans, or anything special to say in a hurry. They had been almost inseparable and this was the first letter she had ever had from him.

Yesterday she might have torn it up unread, but she was less intolerant this morning. Even as she read Kevin's letter her eyes misted over, but she blinked and went on reading. He was missing her badly he said, and if only she would give him the chance he knew they could get back together and it would be even better than it used to be. He reminded her of the good times when they had been happy. She read to the end and sighed then realised that the sisters were looking at her, she must be a sorry sight and she tried to smile.

'Is it your young man?' Flora asked sympathetically.

'Yes.'

They thought she had come up here because her love affair had foundered, so they would understand if she gave this reason for leaving. 'He wants me back.' In a flash their expressions changed from concern to horror.

'Oh no,' said Dora. 'You can't leave us for Christmas. And for New Year's Eve.'

'Did you spend Christmas with him last year.'

After a moment Morag said, 'Yes.' There had been the party at which they had both been guests, although they hadn't started dating until they met again at a supermarket check-out in February and that time clicked on sight. And got on without one angry word until she walked out on him.

After last night she would know better than to pass moral judgments on anyone again. How could she be so sanctimonious when she had clung to Callum quite as eagerly as Kevin had grabbed the girl who shot up from under the sheets with him when Morag appeared in the bedroom door? And with a lot more passion and fervour because Morag would not have heard anyone coming into that tower room if they had been in hob-nailed boots.

'Oh my dear, don't look so woeful,' Flora begged. The sisters were hovering over her. It was sweet of them to care and to want to keep her here, and Callum would probably be away for a few days during which she might even 'phone Kevin.

'Tell us about him,' Dora urged. 'We've often wondered. Is he tall and dark and handsome?'

'He's tall and fair,' said Morag.

'I said he was fair and handsome,' Flora said smugly

so they must have discussed the man they believed had broken her heart. 'Would you have a picture of him?'

'Well, yes I have.'

'I said you would. Do fetch it, and show it to us.'

She supposed she didn't really mind telling them something about Kevin. Perhaps talking would help make up her mind, whether she could take up her old life again, so she went to get the pack of photographs out of her suitcase.

Taken at a midsummer party, each was a colourful little scene. Music had been blaring, everyone had been smiling, Morag hadn't had a care in the world. Kevin was photogenic, the lights caught his fair hair and his eyes were Paul Newman blue and the sisters were thrilled with him. He looked as much the romantic hero as any of the photographs Flora had collected over the years, and now they believed they were in her confidence they asked dozens of questions.

She answered them truthfully. She told them he was an artist, portraits were really his thing, he had been half-way through a painting of Morag when she left him, although sometimes he experimented with abstracts. There had been trouble over another girl, she didn't go into how short and sharp the trouble had been—but that was over now and Kevin wanted Morag to go back to London and to him.

They were not enthusiastic about that. They wanted her to 'phone him, write to him, but not to pack her bags and leave, and when it came out during the day that Callum would not be returning to Calla for at least a week she agreed that perhaps there was no mad hurry.

Kevin's letter could not have been better timed. It had calmed her down amazingly. Now what she had to do was get back to the way she was. A woman with a cool head and some pride. She had made such a fool of herself with Callum, and so far as uninhibited passion went she might be in deep freeze for the rest of her life, and that she could live with.

In retrospect she could be as cynical about their lovemaking as he was. It had been a fantastic sensual sensation because he was a marvellous lover and she had probably been pretty good herself, but never again, thank you.

She decided to send Kevin a Christmas card, thanking him for his letter and saying that she had missed him too. In fact she had hardly given him a thought for weeks, but she was going to start thinking about him again because she needed something to keep Callum out of her mind.

She said, 'I can only stay a few more days, I'm sorry,' and Flora said 'We'll talk about that later shall we? You can't go before Christmas.'

For the next week Morag let things drift. Christmas was only a fortnight away and Callum would not be spending it here. He 'phoned to say he was caught up in some business deals in Brussels and the sisters took it well enough. New Year's Eve was the big occasion, he would be home for that so Morag decided that she might as well stay on over Christmas. The weather was arctic but there was plenty for her to do inside the castle.

A great fir tree was shipped in and hoisted up in the hall, towering above the first storey, and banks of holly and ivy were stacked around. Everybody seemed to know what they were doing, as though this was how the castle was decorated every year.

The sisters were as excited as children, fairly giggling together, and that depressed Morag because it made them seem not so far from second childhood. Although why shouldn't they be thrilled by Christmas? All their lives the festive season would have been a round of parties and although times were changing for them their memories must still give them pleasure.

She herself couldn't work up the slightest spark of enthusiasm. She wished she could have bought gifts that were worth giving, but there was nothing on the island that was likely to delight the Flora-Dora twins, and for the life of her she could think of nothing the Frasers needed. When I leave here she thought. I shall send them gifts, I'll find something for all of them. But while she was still in the castle she couldn't get into the spirit of Christmas, and Christmas morning was like any other winter day with snow swirling outside the window.

The Frasers wished her Merry Christmas and she wished them the same and then she took up the tray. The sisters were in warm winter négligés, Dora in a chair, Flora propped up in bed with Polly beside her. They looked as though they were waiting for Morag as they chorused, 'Merry Christmas.'

'Thank you.'

'There's part of your present,' Flora said. A parcel the shape of a picture, wrapped in scarlet paper dotted with silver hearts, was propped up against Dora's chair.

'I haven't got you anything,' Morag apologised.

'Do *open* it,' Dora enthused and Morag knelt down and began to take off the paper, carefully as though it might be used again. But when she got her first glimpse of the canvas she gasped and began to rip, because this was a painting of her, against a window she knew well.

It was the portrait Kevin had been working on when she left him and she said softly, 'Oh, he sent it, that was kind.'

'Not exactly . . .' Flora began.

Dora finished triumphantly, 'He *brought* it.' The slightly ajar door into the dressing room was pushed wider and Kevin stepped into the room.

CHAPTER SIX

Morag was speechless with astonishment, and with delight because these days she would have welcomed any old friend and Kevin had been the closest of them all. She sat there on the floor, laughing and gasping together, with the sisters clapping hands and even Polly rushing around, wagging her tail.

'How did this happen?' Morag croaked. 'How did you get here?' As Kevin reached her and she jumped up. 'When?'

'Yesterday,' said Kevin.

'We smuggled him in,' said Flora gleefully.

'You knew?' As he was waiting in their dressing room for Morag to walk in with the breakfast tray of course they knew.

'I was invited,' he said, and she looked back at the sisters who were wreathed in smiles, pleased as Punch with themselves.

'By us,' exclaimed Flora.

'We do love a romance,' Dora sighed and Morag thought what a shock it would have been to them if she had said—it wasn't Kevin's letter that made me want to get away from here, it was because the castle isn't big enough for Callum and me. Come to that, neither is the island.

'Now you take him downstairs,' said Dora, 'and get him some breakfast.'

'Do the Frasers know?'

'Hamish brought Kevin up from the harbour yesterday afternoon,' Flora explained.

On Christmas Eve there had been comings and goings all day at the castle. But the idea of Hamish and Mrs

Fraser as conspirators hurrying Kevin into his hiding place, keeping him out of Morag's way was comic.

She was smiling about that, shaking her head in amazement, as she and Kevin came out of the bedroom and began to walk down the long draughty corridor.

'Is there a map of this place?' he asked. 'How do you find your way?'

'I'll draw you one. Till then you'll just have to follow me.'

'You bet I'll follow you. I won't let you out of my sight.'

When he took her in his arms she hugged him back and said, 'Oh it is *good* to see you.' He kissed her and she thought—I have missed him. We had good times together. Now it won't be so bad here with someone to share the laughs. And she looked up over his shoulder and the portrait on the wall was the scowling life-size full-length one of the bearded seventeenth century Maconnell with Callum's eyes.

She found herself drawing back from the embrace, linking arms instead and saying gaily, 'This is a conspiracy. How did it happen?'

'Well this bloke in pin-striped trousers turned up and said was I Kevin Sanders and would I like to spend Christmas and the New Year at Calla Castle, all expenses paid and everything arranged. Only not to tell anybody who could tell you because it was a surprise.'

'You can say that again,' said Morag.

'And would I finish the painting I was doing of you and bring it along together with my paints. They looked at it last night before they gift-wrapped it, asked what I charged and said I could paint them while I was here.'

'Lovely,' said Morag. That might lead to other commissions and couldn't be bad. Kevin was getting his first real look around and finding it impressive and overpowering.

'How about this place? It's like something out of Macbeth. There must be money here.'

'Mmm. Does——' she hesitated for a moment, 'does Callum know you're here?'

'Who?'

'Callum Maconnell, he's the Master of Calla. He hired me as their companion.'

Kevin looked blank. 'Nobody mentioned him.' Then he grinned. 'But the double-act seem very fond of you. Sisters are they?'

'Twins,' said Morag, and thought it unlikely that Callum's permission had been sought or that Callum would care. After all what was one more guest in a place this size?

They reached the top of the great staircase, and Kevin's neck swivelled as he took in paintings and tapestries and hunting trophies and armour; and finally the two Great Danes.

'They're another double act,' said Morag. 'Jekyll and Hyde. Hyde bites, and it's hard to tell them apart until he does.'

Kevin skirted both dogs as he followed her to the breakfast room. This was rarely used but the kitchens were going to be busy enough on Christmas Day without cluttering them up further. In the summer the windows overlooked terraced gardens but now they framed a bleak picture glimpsed through swirling snow. 'Do you ever get snowed in?' Kevin was shivering.

'They should have warned you to pack thick sweaters. We don't get snowed in because the winds never let the snow settle, but most winters the island gets cut off. He turned from the window still shivering but smiling. 'That mightn't be so bad. They've given me a bedroom near yours, we can keep each other warm.'

She wished the sisters had consulted her. She was all for Kevin coming for Christmas but rooms too close was taking too much for granted, and she would not be rushed, she was done with impetuosity. 'I'll see about breakfast,' she said. 'Don't go away.'

Mrs Fraser was still in the kitchen, dressed in her usual black but this dress had lace cuffs and a collar pinned with a large cameo brooch. She wore a bibbed white apron and she was already at the sink, preparing vegetables. 'Did you know about this?' she asked as Morag walked in.

'I hadn't a clue,' Morag laughed. 'I got the surprise of my life. I don't even know how they got his address.' Maybe off the Christmas card, her cards had gone in with the sisters' to be taken away and mailed. Or even from Kevin's letter, she wouldn't put it past them to have searched for that, they weren't overburdened with scruples.

'They do get some airy-fairy notions,' said Mrs Fraser. 'Hamish said to me last night "I hope the lassie likes the lad because she won't have much chance of getting away from him now they've shipped him up here."'

And put him in a room near to mine, Morag thought, but she could hardly start by making an issue of that. 'Yes I like him,' she said.

Mrs Fraser was quite human this morning, after all it was Christmas Day. She had ham and sausages ready, and Morag fried a couple of eggs and filled a plate. She wasn't ready for a heavy meal herself, there would be a lot of eating to do later, but she put toast in the rack, butter and marmalade on the tray.

Mrs Fraser was curious about Kevin, all the Frasers had been told was that he had to be collected from the harbour and smuggled into the castle and up to a bedroom and fed, and Morag was not to know because this was a Christmas surprise for her.

It had seemed a funny business at the time but it was nice for Morag to have a friend of her own here over the holiday, Mrs Fraser had noticed but not mentioned that the girl had been peaky lately. She asked openly who Kevin was and where he came from. Once Morag told her she said, 'He's a good looking lad,' and in a flush of Christmas generosity added, 'You make a bonny pair.'

Morag smiled and said, 'Thank you,' and picked up the tray and checked an impulse to deny that she and Kevin were a pair. They were friends, good mates again, but separate, although she was really glad he was here.

She carried the tray to the breakfast room and found him examining the pictures. They were mostly darkish oil paintings of rugged scenery, but he was standing in front of a lady who had sat for the artist in the large drawing room downstairs over a hundred years ago. The drawing room had hardly changed and Kevin was chewing his underlip. 'It's a bit old fashioned isn't it? They won't be expecting me to turn out anything like this will they?'

His work was simpler, modern, concentrating less on detail, and Morag said, 'They've seen your style, they must like it. Come and eat.'

He sat down and reached for a knife and fork. 'I'm ravenous. It must be the air, I could eat a horse.'

She nibbled on toast and they chattered like old times. It was not the first time they had breakfasted together and the misunderstanding that had come between them was never mentioned. Morag felt that she had over-reacted. Sex could be a kind of mindless madness and she knew that now.

Kevin thought she was forgiving him because she had missed him, and she wasn't going to admit that if she had kept up any resentment it would have been a case of the pot calling the kettle black. So it was all sweetness and light and no one could have given her a better Christmas present than Kevin come to stay.

Callers came, bringing gifts and greetings and going

away with presents from under the great tree in the hall. The sisters held court in the large drawing room, Flora with her feet up on a silver-grey brocade sofa and Dora in a throne-like chair with a footstool. The crystal chandeliers were lit and huge fires burned in the two white marble fireplaces. The snow kept falling but it was still possible to get around the island and all morning cars were drawing in and out of the courtyard.

None of the callers had come to see Morag and she kept in the background. She was in charge of Hyde, who was antisocial enough to take a piece out of a visitor even on Christmas Day. Hyde was confined to the brewhouse, a room leading off the kitchens that hadn't been used for fifty years. That was the extent of her duties. Nobody else had anything for her to do, so she wandered around with Kevin, and was glad of his company.

There was plenty to show him. The ballroom knocked him sidewards. He literally swayed when she ushered him into that vast empty room with the minstrels' gallery up there in the shadows. 'What do they use this for?' he asked. 'Indoor football? You could get a full size pitch in here.'

'It's the ballroom.' Six days from now it would be the brightest and busiest room in the castle. 'They have a New Year's Eve Ball,' she said. 'I wasn't planning to be here. I thought I'd leave as soon as Christmas was over.'

'Of course you'll leave,' Kevin put an arm about her neck and kissed her mouth, 'you'll leave with me but it might be a laugh to stay on for the ball.'

She didn't care either way. 'If you like,' she said. 'Do you want me to teach you how to dance a reel?'

She danced in the middle of the empty floor, smiling, pushing and pulling Kevin through the routines. He was a good mover, a good dancer, and every so often he grabbed her and kissed her and they laughed together and afterwards they sat on the steps leading up to the gallery while Kevin got his breath back. 'What have you done to your hair?' he asked suddenly.

'It frizzes up here. It always used to during the winter. You don't like it?'

'It's wild,' he said.

'Thanks.' And her eyes were on one of the doors at the far end of the room. A closed door that led to the north wing, where all her wildness was locked away.

Christmas dinner was traditional fare, turkey and trimmings, Christmas pudding and brandy butter. Flora sat at the bottom of the table and Dora to the right of the empty seat at the top: and down the long gleaming table, with its silverware and shining glasses, sat the Frasers, and Fergus from the lodge and Kevin and Morag with plenty of elbow room. Morag reckoned the table could have taken over twenty comfortably and wondered why they didn't all move up to one end and why the chair at the top that had to be Callum's was left so ostentatiously empty.

It was an irritation, because while it stood there she kept half expecting him to walk into the room and apologise for being late, and sit down and look at her with that piercing stare that made her feel as though he was touching her.

The wine flowed. The Frasers were fairly abstemious but Fergus from the lodge quaffed heartily and the sisters sipped away, and Kevin drank a few glasses. Morag was sure the bottles were a good vintage, it tasted very pleasant, especially the champagne, and by the end of the meal everyone was well fed and happy.

Then it was time for the sisters' siesta. Doctor's orders that nothing must disrupt. Morag went up with them and while she helped them slip off their shoes and loosen their dresses she thanked them for inviting Kevin.

Dora flopped on to the bed with a grunt. 'I hope the

brandy butter isn't going to disagree with me. He seems a nice young man.'

'Yes he is,' said Morag.

'We couldn't have you dashing off,' said Flora, settling herself into her pillows. 'We thought you'd like him here for Christmas and the New Year and we thought if you had a little time together it would help you decide whether you really do want to go back to him.'

Morag wasn't sure now whether they wanted a love story with a happy ending or for her to have second thoughts and stay with them. 'There's cunning,' she said and the sisters giggled and Flora hiccuped delicately.

Of course Morag was leaving Calla. She couldn't stay on here and today with Kevin had reminded her how well they did get on together. He really was a lovely man, with his fair waving hair, his regular features and his slim taut-muscled body.

He was waiting for her in the hall and she said, 'Let's go in here,' and led the way into the small drawing room. The Frasers had a parlour of their own, they and Fergus would probably have retired to that. Later Morag would help clear away, and feed dishes into the dishwasher, but surely everyone was entitled to an hour's relaxation after Christmas dinner. She was glad to find the room empty, this seemed like the first time today they had been alone. Kevin closed the door as he followed her and she went into his arms and he said, 'Angel-baby don't ever run away from me again.'

His eyes were blue and it was crazy that they should seem shallow, but then she was comparing them with eyes that were dark and deep as the pit, and her lips twitched at being called baby when she had this feeling that she was not only taller but stronger. She was not taller, it was just that Kevin, five years older, seemed so very young and she kissed him hard, desperately trying to work up a little genuine passion.

It would have gone beyond kisses. He showered them on her face, fumbling with the zip down the back of her dress and getting it stuck almost at once and she moved towards the sofa, telling herself—I love him and I need him. He can give me back my pride because he loves me, and as Mrs Fraser says we make a bonny pair.

The door opened and Mrs Fraser stood there, smiling. 'Aren't you going to come and watch the Queen's speech with us?' she said.

It was an invitation into their parlour, the first Morag had had, and it would have been unkind to refuse although Kevin was starting, 'Well, I'm not much——' 'Oh yes,' Morag said. She pulled an apologetic face as they walked down the corridor behind Mrs Fraser, and mouthed 'Tonight' and Kevin grinned ruefully.

There were a number of 'phone calls during the day, all for the sisters but the one from Alistair for Morag. She had had a Christmas card from him and she had sent him one, with a line to say that she was all right, but the 'phone call was welcome. He sounded anxious about her, and she told him that Callum was away and that Kevin was there with her. 'I'm having a lovely Christmas,' she said. 'Things couldn't be better, honestly. Wasn't that a smashing Christmas present, them inviting Kevin up here?'

The sisters had another gift for her. During the evening, they brought out a pair of antique filigree earrings set with tiny pearls and diamonds, and after her involuntary exclamation of delight her first thought was—they've got to be heirlooms, what's Callum going to say about this? She was not sure she could accept them but the kindness of the gesture touched her, and come to that so did Mrs Fraser's gift of a pair of bright green hand-knitted leg warmers. She should have been giving gifts and she stammered her apologies and Mrs Fraser said shrewdly, 'You haven't been feeling much like Christmas have you? You haven't been yourself lately.'

Today she was herself again, lively and laughing. Sitting with the sisters and Kevin, Christmas night there was more eating and drinking and Kevin held her hand, and put his arm along the back of the sofa behind her and it was all cosy and comforting. He was going to start on the sisters' portrait tomorrow and tonight he and Morag would be alone together and she couldn't believe she had ever walked out on him when they suited each other so well.

At ten o'clock Flora said, 'Well children it's bedtime for us.' The 'phone rang almost simultaneously. Dora picked up the extension and said happily, '*Callum*,' and Morag was jolted out of her dream as though she had been dropped into icy water. She never moved while Dora told him that they had had a very pleasant very quiet Christmas Day, and then Flora took the 'phone and said much the same, but every nerve in Morag was suddenly strung to screaming pitch.

'Have a word with Morag,' said Flora and Morag walked across and wanted to run and grab the 'phone.

'Hello,' she said, in a light cool voice, 'had a good Christmas?' She wanted to ask, 'What are you doing? Where are you? Who's with you? When are you coming back?'

'Yes,' he said. 'How did yours go?' That was it. Just a brief exchange of clichés. But the deep slow voice of the man who was miles away was turning her on more than Kevin's kisses had. Her heart was racing and her blood was tingling. When he said, 'I'll see you next Saturday,' she said 'We'll be here,' and the pips came and she hung up then looked at the sisters. 'I'm sorry, did you want to say anything else?'

'We'd finished,' said Flora, 'although I suppose we might have told him Kevin was here.' She smiled at Kevin. 'That was my grandson,' she explained. 'You'll meet him next weekend.'

I suppose I could have told him about Kevin thought Morag, but while she could hear Callum's voice nobody else had existed. One thing was sure. She couldn't let another man make love to her while this obsession raged in her, and tonight's excuse was to hand, the rich food and the mixed drinks were making her squeamish. That and the shock of realising how badly she was hooked on Callum. If he hadn't 'phoned she would have gone happily to bed.

She went upstairs with the sisters and saw them into their beds. In their parlour the Frasers and Old Fergus sat reminiscing about old Christmasses over glasses of dark pungent liquor. Morag said good night to them and no thank you she didn't think she'd try a dram of the punch. Jekyll and Hyde were prowling around and Kevin was still where she had left him on the sofa. He yawned when she walked in and she guessed he had dozed for the last half hour. He had had a busy couple of days.

She said, 'I think the champagne's caught up with the *marrons glacés.* I'm going to bed with a handful of Alka Seltzers. Can you find your way to your room?'

His face fell. 'I'd rather find my way to yours.'

'Sorry.' She was sorry. It would have been so much easier if she and Kevin could have slipped back into the old relationship, but what had seemed simple enough an hour ago was impossible now.

At his door he kissed her, trying to draw her in. She resisted gently, if he had used strength so would she because she was going nowhere with him, finally he said reluctantly, 'Go and take your Alka Seltzers and get an hour or two's sleep.'

She didn't question that. She said good night and locked her bedroom door, and lay there feeling genuinely queasy. But she was asleep when she heard the rattle of the door handle and the tap on the door. She woke and listened and the tapping went on. There was no way she was going to open her door for Kevin so he could rattle away. He wouldn't dare make too much noise for fear of disturbing the sisters.

Next morning he said, 'You must have been out like the dead last night. I knocked on your door.'

'Did you?' She looked at him, wide-eyed. 'I should have warned you about walking in the night because the dogs don't know you.'

Kevin's eyes narrowed. 'What's changed you? You weren't for setting the dogs on me yesterday.'

She had just taken in the sisters' breakfast tray and met him coming down the corridor and they were walking together now towards the staircase. She said, 'I was very glad to see you yesterday, I'm still glad to see you of course but it was a complete surprise and I think it scattered my wits because now I know I'm not ready to take up again, not the way we were. Friends O.K. but if you won't settle for that for now maybe you'd better see if you can get back to the mainland. Although it seems a shame to miss the portrait commission.'

A dull flush rose in Kevin's face. 'Thanks for nothing,' he said, but he could do with the commission they both knew that. It was the frustration of Morag's retreat when yesterday she had seemed so willing that was choking him. Sulkily he said, 'It's been a long time.'

She drawled, 'I'm sure you didn't take a vow of celibacy after I left.'

'That's got nothing to do with it.'

No, he could have had a dozen women and it would have been nothing to her, and she said, 'Maybe you can make a holiday of it and like you say the New Year's Eve Ball should be a laugh.'

He was not placated. He hunched his shoulders and dug his hands into his pockets and said, 'On probation then am I? Well I'd better get on with painting the two old trout.'

An easel was brought down from the schoolroom and set up in the drawing room and the sisters were posed side by side on the silver-grey brocade sofa. They were not good sitters. 'It was easier last time,' said Flora sighing at the memory of eighteen-year-old suppleness compared with her arthritic hip and Dora sighed too, and they both shifted position and Kevin swore under his breath. But their low boredom threshold was the major obstacle. Within half an hour they were obviously bored stiff, longing to call the whole thing off, and Morag asked desperately, 'Do you have any photographs?'

Kevin often painted from photographs and he jumped at the suggestion. They found him pictures of themselves at all ages and he took paints and easel back to the schoolroom where Morag laid the fire and Kevin pinned a montage of faces on to a faded green baize wall-board.

The schoolroom made an adequate studio, with windows high and wide enough to let in light, even on a winter's day. Morag wondered if Callum had taken lessons in here, sitting at the table, a tutor at the desk. He had been away at school when his parents were killed, he had only been seven then so he would have been very young if this had ever been his schoolroom. It was hard to imagine him as a child.

There was coal dust on her hands but the wood had caught and the fire was burning and she rubbed her fingers on a tissue and thought that she could see a boy in her mind with Callum's eyes and hair. His son that Flora and Dora were waiting for so eagerly, Rosalie's child, and pain stabbed at her. Kevin was talking and she said, 'What?'

'Your picture, I want it in here.'

He sounded as if she had gone deaf and so she had for a moment. 'Next best thing to having you here.' He liked his work. He had no great talent, but he enjoyed putting paint on canvas, and he would be getting a good price for this, and he had no doubt that Morag would come round before long. He grinned at her, blowing on his fingernails. 'And keep the fire going will you or I'll be down with frostbite.'

'I will,' she promised, and she came out of the schoolroom, with the relief of a schoolmarm whose troublesome pupil is occupied for a while.

She did have trouble with Kevin. When he was near her he couldn't keep his hands off her. He pawed and patted, stroking her cheek or her hand, as they sat over meals or in the evening. Even with fires burning in the rooms that were used it was so cold that there wasn't much else he could stroke without Morag's co-operation, and she spent the week in heavy sweaters and skirts and thick ribbed tights, and the nights with her bedroom door locked. Touching was no turn-on as far as she was concerned, and Kevin simmered with increasing frustration as New Year's Eve drew nearer.

Preparing the food for all the guests who had been invited put the kitchens back to the days when all the castle was occupied and staff swarmed everywhere. Mrs Fraser had a small army of local helpers and Morag did whatever she was asked, enjoying the bustle and the fuss, although every day brought a few cancellations in the guest list.

That was because of the weather. It was a threatening week of thunderous skies and mountainous seas and Morag couldn't blame anyone who was unwilling to take the trip out to Calla. She remembered Callum saying there might only be the Frasers, the sisters, Morag and himself and anyone else who could stagger up the hill, and stagger could be the word because the gales never dropped. Enough food to feed a regiment and maybe even the pipers and the fiddlers wouldn't get through.

The sisters tutted over the apologies and excuses but

most of the guests were obviously leaving it till the day and hoping for the best; and they were having a lovely time choosing the dresses and jewellery they would wear and getting into the swing of the preparations.

Morag's dress had been a small problem. She had nothing remotely suitable for a ball with her, and while she was helping Flora and Dora go through their top-designer evening wear—they hoarded like squirrels, the styles went back about fifty years—she asked hesitantly, 'I wonder, please, could I borrow something?'

If it was only a pretty blouse and an Indian cashmere scarf it would make all the difference, but they insisted, immediately and together, that she take anything she wanted. 'Perhaps you are slightly taller than us,' Dora conceded, 'but your mother was such a clever needlewomen I'm sure you could do a little alteration.'

Morag wished she was seven inches shorter. There was a peacock-blue chiffon from their 'flapper' days she would have loved to wear, but there was no way she could lengthen that to anything but a very short shift; and in the end she took a shot-silk in orange and russets with a high frilled neck and leg-o-mutton sleeves. The sash was wide and long enough to put another flounce on the bottom of the rustling skirt, and it was a romantic dreamy dress. She sewed in the little room off the kitchen, as her mother had done, and the sisters were enchanted when she put it on for them.

Nobody else saw it. She went from their bedroom to hers and looked at herself in the mirror, and held her hair up from her face, the way she would dress it, and knew that she was doing all this for Callum. Rosalie was coming to the ball of course, although Morag told herself that she wasn't bothered about Rosalie. But other women would be there, debutantes, glamorous jet-setters, real competition. Morag would need all the help she could get, because nothing before had ever mattered so much to her as being the girl Callum turned

to first when the new year came in, because that would
mean the new year was theirs . . .

On New Year's Eve the winds dropped. Temperatures
were still sub-zero but it meant that guests had a good
chance of reaching the castle, and the sisters were as
smug as if they had personally fixed it. By afternoon
guests had started arriving and the castle was taking on
the atmosphere of a family hotel, as newcomers were
ushered into the large drawing room to be greeted by
the sisters, while their luggage was carted up to their
overnight rooms.

So far Morag had recognised nobody, but they all
seemed to know each other and she knew she was the
outsider. She didn't try to be anything else. She carried
cases, and did what the Frasers asked her to do, and the
sisters wouldn't need her until it was time for them to
get dressed for the ball.

Her constant charge was Hyde. She kept him by her,
and when she couldn't she locked him in the brewhouse
with Jekyll for company.

Kevin worked in the schoolroom for most of that
day. Morag took him up a tray of food at lunchtime
and there he stayed. The painting was coming along
and the sisters were anxious it should be as near
complete as possible when Callum saw it. Nobody knew
what time to expect Callum. He was bringing two guests
with him but neither was Rosalie. She was coming with
her parents and Morag hadn't seen the family arrive.

All day Morag had the evening on her mind. In
Flora's dress, with her hair styled and in full glamour,
Callum would think she was beautiful. They would
dance together, talk. He would have had time to realise
that what he had overheard on the 'phone had no
bearing at all on what had happened in the north
wing, and everything would be wonderful. Tonight she
would be sensational. She couldn't have been looking

forward to it more if the ball had been her own personal date with Callum, she was so convinced that nothing would come between them.

She looked into the schoolroom when the light was fading, to see how the painting was going. Even with black skies the light up here was cold and clear for a few hours each day, but Kevin had turned on the lights and was working against the clock. It wouldn't be finished but it was the sisters all right and Morag said, 'It's good,' and stayed to watch for a few minutes and talk about what was going on in the rest of the castle.

'There's a whole batch of them come over on the car ferry—and that hasn't been able to run for a couple of weeks so we're lucky there, and some are anchored around the island and Hamish keeps muttering "They're gettin' in y'ken, I hope they'll be gettin' oot". And the fiddlers are tuning up in the ballroom although there's another three hours to go before the dancing starts.'

Her cheeks and eyes were glowing, she was electric with excitement, and Kevin put down brush and palette and tried to pull her closer. She didn't resist. The mood she was in she could have hugged him from sheer joy of life, and she knew he was going to enjoy himself tonight. There would be plenty of pretty girls around. 'I want every dance with you.' he said, and she smiled. 'You haven't seen what's come. I promise you'll be spoilt for choice.'

'I've made my choice.' He buried his face in her hair. The sisters walked in and Flora had her arm through Callum's.

Morag's heart missed a beat and then started pounding like mad, and again there was that weird feeling that everything and everyone but Callum were fading into a mist.

'Hello,' he said.

'Hello,' said Morag.

The two old women introduced Kevin. 'We've told him all about you,' said Flora, coming out of the mist smiling, Morag wanted to protest because everything the sisters would have told Callum about Kevin would be wrong. She must tell him how things really were. That Kevin's visit was one of the Flora-Dora twins' airy-fairy notions because, goodness knows, Morag had not been pining for him.

Kevin grinned, and Callum inspected the painting and said it was interesting. Morag saw it through his eyes and knew that it wasn't outstanding; and she looked at the two men and felt like Cathy comparing Heathcliff and Edgar Linton. The longing for Callum was a physical ache. He wasn't even looking her way. His back was turned to her, but the shoulders and even the way his hair grew filled her with such yearning that if he had smiled at her she would have gone to him and at least put her hands on him and maybe kissed him in front of them all.

From the painting of the sisters he turned to the painting of Morag. That was perched on a chair so that it faced Kevin as he worked, and it was a better picture. The subject was easier of course, but he had caught a mood of languor that was intimate and provocative. She lounged on a window seat, long bare legs gracefully sprawled, bare arms folded behind her head. She wore a brief and shapeless white shirt, her hair was loose and from her smile and her heavy lidded eyes she could have just rolled out of bed. She hadn't in fact, not at any of the sittings, but it was one of the sexiest portraits Kevin had ever produced and he was proud of it.

Callum laughed and said, 'So that's what she looks like under the wrappings. You're a lucky man.' As though he had never seen her, touched her, and her face flamed and the sisters pretended to be shocked at the suggestion that this was a near-naked study.

Kevin said, 'I know it.'

'I can explain,' Morag said aloud to her empty bedroom. It was almost time for the guests to head towards the ballroom. She had spent a good hour with the sisters, and left them both looking quite splendid in gowns that must have cost a fortune, Flora's ruby-red and Dora's midnight blue, and enough jewellery to rival the chandeliers. The last forty minutes she had worked on herself.

Morag had always been fairly satisfied with her own appearance. At her best she could have men spinning around in the street for a second look but she was not so sure she was going to shine tonight when it mattered so much. Even the dress she had chosen could be a mistake. Although it was one of the few that could be altered to fit her there was nothing very eyecatching about it, and now, a week too late, she started wondering if there might have been any way she could have lengthened the blue chiffon.

She would have liked to wear the antique earrings but another small problem was how Callum would react to that gift. The blessed things had probably been in his family for centuries, and she had enough explaining to do. So she chose pearls instead, large lustrous drop pearls dangling from thin gold chains, and probably the only fake jewellery that would be worn tonight.

The excitement that had been buoying her up all day had vanished in those few minutes in the schoolroom. She had been fooling herself that Callum would be as glad to see her as she was to see him, and that the joy of being together again would be all that mattered. She hadn't wanted him to see her first in her thick warm everyday clothes, she had wanted to be dressed for the ball like a scene from a period novel. Although now she realised that it would have been more sensible to have listened for the helicopter and got to him before the sisters did.

Then at least she could have said, 'I hope you don't

mind but your grandmother and your great-aunt brought a visitor up for Christmas. A man I knew in London. I knew nothing about it until he popped up on Christmas morning. If they'd asked me if I wanted him here I'd have told them not to bother.'

Once Callum had walked out of that room she hadn't been able to catch him. He had gone with the sisters and she had been held back for a few moments by Kevin who said, 'I don't suppose much gets in his way and lives to tell the tale. All the same I'd like the chance of painting him.'

'I don't think——' Morag had begun. She didn't want Kevin snubbed and she knew how Callum would react to that suggestion.

'Neither do I' said Kevin.

She did follow, but Callum always seemed to be talking to at least half a dozen folk at once and he never seemed to look her way. She tried the trick of willing him to look, while she was collecting empty coffee cups in the huge drawing room, because if she could just catch his eye she could smile and maybe give a little grimace that would mean, 'Please, I'd like a minute, I've things to say.'

But he never turned his head and she carried the tray of cups to the kitchen. Most of the guests thought she was staff, as indeed she was, and talked across and through her as if she was invisible.

'Have you seen Rosalie Perry?' one blonde asked another as Morag passed them and they both peered around. Then both began to giggle as the second one said, 'She'll be here if she has to swim to Calla. Will this be the year she gets him?'

'Not if I can help it,' said the first, who looked as if no expense had been spared on her since the day she was born, and Morag supposed that Callum would be as eligible as any man here tonight and she herself would be lucky if she could get near him . . .

Even now she still felt far from confident. She hoped she looked good. She stood in front of her bedroom mirror, hands on her hips and shoulders back, red hair coiled and pinned, gold-green eyeshadow emphasising the grass green eyes, a dusting of gold on her cheekbones highlighting the lovely bone structure of her face. But for all her defiant stance she was scared.

When the knock came on the door, just before eight, she stood still. It would be Kevin, they were going down together, but, for three seconds she froze with closed eyes and as she walked slowly to answer it she was praying that it might be Callum, who would say, 'I've come for you.'

But she wasn't disappointed to see Kevin standing there, saying, 'You look lovely,' because she had known it wouldn't be Callum. Kevin had packed for the celebrations and was wearing a black velvet suit and a pink shirt and Morag said, 'So do you. Shall we go?'

In medieval times the ballroom had been the great hall, the heart of the castle. Minstrels had played their roundelays in the minstrels' gallery while down below the Maconnells and their allies had eaten huge meals at long tables, arranged marriages and reared children; plotted and gone out to battle. And had wild carousals, this room had seen a few orgies in its time.

The clans were here in force tonight. At least half the men were wearing the kilt, and a fair number of women had tartan sashes pinned diagonally from shoulder to hip.

Not the sisters. They wanted no scarves hiding their jewellery as they waited with Callum at the far end of the room, flanked by two suits of armour and under a huge protrait of Bonnie Prince Charlie, to greet their guests. Most of the guests had been welcomed earlier but there was still a path for latecomers through the chattering crowds.

Morag couldn't take her eyes off Callum. In full

regalia of velvet doublet and kilt, with his thatch of black hair and strong arrogant face he could have stepped right up there into the picture beside the man who was standing in the heather.

Kevin had an arm around her waist and she hardly felt it, she was so intent on Callum. In the minstrels' gallery they were setting the scene with a selection of Burns songs. A baritone was singing, 'So deep in love am I, that I will love thee still my dear when all the seas run dry,' and she thought, yes, I am so deep in love that there's no hope for me unless I can get to you.

Look at me she willed him, *look at me*. It hadn't worked before but she would go on trying and sometime tonight he was going to look and see her. When they were face to face he would see that she was beautiful.

She watched Flora, who was seated in a chair like a small throne, reach up to touch his arm and speak to him, smiling, and she heard Kevin say, in tones of awe, 'What a fantastic girl.'

Morag turned then to see a girl on the arm of a distinguished looking silver-haired man, walking down the ballroom. A hush settled. She was wearing a white dress, cut to show one smooth white shoulder. She had a tiny waist, swelling breasts, and her shining fair hair was in a chin length bob, waving back. She looked soft and sweet, exuding the devastating sexual aura of a young Marilyn Monroe.

It was several seconds before Morag recognised Rosalie. Rosalie had had the same idea as Morag. Tonight she was going to be irresistible. And she was. She was no child tonight. She was the woman who was causing a ripple of admiration to run through this sophisticated gathering, and Callum came to meet her, looking at her with incredulity, and a tenderness that Morag felt was a certain starter for love . . .

CHAPTER SEVEN

IT was no use now Morag trying to explain about Kevin, or telling Callum that she had missed him dreadfully, because this was Rosalie's night.

'You think I couldn't seduce him?' Rosalie had said to Morag. The way she looked now she could probably seduce any man with blood in his veins and jealousy hit Morag with a knife blow. She had been holding an untouched drink for the last ten minutes, now she gulped it down and Kevin asked, 'Who is she? Do you know?'

'Her name's Rosalie Perry, working her way to being Rosalie Maconnell.' Morag kept her voice low and amused, and waited for the pain because after that first savage stab she felt numb.

The couple who had to be Rosalie's parents, were talking to the sisters and Callum, and then they moved away to greet somebody else. Rosalie stayed where she was because Dora held her there, and that showed all of them that Rosalie was more than a friend, she was family. She made up the group that welcomed the stragglers and Morag turned away because she couldn't bear to watch any more.

A few minutes later the baritone came to a throbbing finale and got a round of applause and they were exhorted, 'Ladies and gentlemen take your partners for the first eightsome reel.'

'I'm going to make a mess of this,' said Kevin, facing Morag, and looking at the other three couples who plainly knew what they were about.

'You can't go wrong,' said Morag. An accordionist up in the gallery was getting into the swing, and dancers were tapping their feet. There were ten eightsomes. Almost everyone was being drawn into this send-off for the ball, except Flora whose dancing days were over but who sat on her little throne, radiant with happiness.

Morag knew why. It was because Callum and Rosalie were partnering each other and it was all working out. Tonight he would admit that the sisters knew best, Rosalie had been waiting for him all these years and tonight he would wonder if he had been waiting for her.

Thank God they're at the other end of the room thought Morag, I don't believe I could dance by him without saying, 'I told you she'd get older but it's all on the outside, she's still about fifty years younger than you in the head.' Much good that would do, and she wouldn't say anything, although if they clasped hands she might just possibly hang on to him.

'You're doing well,' everyone encouraged Kevin as he skipped to the right and then to the left, and advanced and retreated; Morag was surprised to find she remembered all the steps because she had danced no reels since she left Calla. But she moved naturally to the old tunes and when the reel ended in a wild gallop she moved back against the wall with Kevin's arm around her waist, laughing up at him.

'I haven't danced one of those for years,' she said. Never here in the castle. At ceilidhs—parties, gatherings that were held in the old days. She had been a child then but a quick and graceful dancer, and one of her dreams had been to go to a ball at the castle. Now she was here she wished she were a thousand miles away.

Kevin, gasping for breath, took a glass from a silver tray that was being carried along by one of the helpers brought in for the occasion. He was Maggie MacTavish's husband and he grinned at Morag and she winked back.

'How long can they go on dancing like that?' asked Kevin.

Morag said gaily, 'New Year's Eve in Scotland can go on for days.' She wouldn't last beyond midnight. After that she could creep away and tomorrow she would face what had to be faced, but until midnight she had to keep smiling and dancing.

A tune from the top ten followed the reel and the ballroom filled with dancers interpreting it their way, some cheek to cheek, others discoing.

'This is more my style,' said Kevin and he and Morag took the floor with a verve that had the pins slipping out of her hair. She had often danced with Kevin, they were good partners on a dance floor, and she kept her eyes on him because that way there was no risk of her looking round and seeing Callum.

If he was dancing with Rosalie in his arms she didn't know that she wouldn't tap his shoulder and say, 'Is this an "Excuse me?"' and if she did she was sure Rosalie would tighten her hold and smile and say, 'No it isn't. You stay with the one you've got.'

She thought Callum might raise an eyebrow, because what with the reel and this dance her hair was falling down, and when the music ended she took out more of the pins and dropped them into a seasonal arrangement of holly that was banked up around one of the pillars.

The long dining room led off the ballroom. This was where they had had Christmas dinner and tonight it was resplendent as a buffet. Morag and Kevin wandered along filling their plates, and found themselves a couple of chairs in a corner. 'They know how to do things don't they?' said Kevin. 'What's this?'

'Some sort of game pie.' Morag leaned over his shoulder. 'They shoot them too you know. Haven't you seen the pictures of all these stags at bay?'

But she couldn't eat, her stomach lurched as she pushed the food around with her fork. When a girl came up and asked, 'Aren't you here to paint the Flora-Doras?' Morag said, 'He is and he's terrific. Would you like to see?' and as Kevin looked at her she said, 'I'll be around, I haven't started on my pie.'

She left the plate under her chair and wandered back into the ballroom where a young man with freckles, wearing the white, yellow, black and blue tartan of the Gordons, asked her to dance.

It was another reel. They faced each other in two long rows, advancing and retreating on each other, but none of them was Callum, and she saw him and Rosalie standing with the onlookers and she waved and whirled by. But he hadn't seen her. She was just one of the crowd of dancers. I wish I had worn the red dress she thought, I wish I had never come back to Calla.

She couldn't have said afterwards with certainty who her own partners were, but there were plenty of them. When they asked her name she said, 'Morag Macdonald'. Some of them had heard of her, some hadn't. When she got no reaction she told them she lived in London—she probably would again after she left here—then she got them talking about themselves and hardly listened to a word they said.

The ones who had heard of her asked, 'You're the—er—the companion?' which meant that the rumour that Callum had installed a girlfriend in the castle had reached them.

She smiled and said, 'Well it all depends what you mean by companion,' and danced on.

Most of the guests here tonight had known each other for ever, their families had been friends for generations. The ballroom was like a village hall for gossip. They knew that the sisters had earmarked Rosalie Perry for Callum, although Callum Maconnell was older and a world more experienced. But tonight Rosalie was beautiful. Tonight they could see it all happening, Rosalie with Callum.

Morag seemed to hear the names from all sides through the music and the babble of voices. Look at them, everyone seemed to be saying, but Morag was not looking. That she couldn't do. She could dance, she could talk, she could laugh, but looking for Callum with Rosalie was beyond her.

She kept moving, keeping up her act of having a wonderful time. When the brigadier stepped up and asked, 'May I have this dance?' and added, 'You're looking enchanting as ever,' she wondered—who the hell is this?

Then the bristling moustache and the red face struck a chord and she remembered him. She had seen Sir Charles and Lady Ensor. He was Dora's admirer, the third of the small party that had come for a few days a few weeks ago. 'Lovely to see you again,' she said.

This was a waltz, slow and dreamy. Morag would have preferred another reel. She did not fancy being encircled by the brigadier but there was no help for it, and the brigadier stepped out, holding her stiffly.

It couldn't be long till midnight. Her head was beginning to ache, and her partner was droning on. She murmured suitable exclamations without paying much attention until she realised he was waiting for an answer and he had just asked her, 'What *are* your plans?'

'Plans?' she echoed.

'Well you can hardly stay on here can you m'dear? A little bird told me there'll be an announcement very soon, and then—well ...' That knowing look meant that Callum's future wife was not going to want his ex-mistress around, and anger burned in her at the cheek of this prejudiced little twit. She'd give them another explanation, something else to think about. 'I shall be leaving as soon as my work's finished,' she said airily. 'I shouldn't be telling you this, but I'm sure you can keep a secret. I'm a journalist. Here to write the story of the Flora-Dora twins. Do you know,' she whispered in his ear, 'they've drawers full of letters, they've kept *everything*.' She giggled, sounding tipsy although fury was sobering her.

He missed a couple of steps and she stood back, smiling, until he steadied himself. Then he cleared his throat. 'For—publication?'

'But of course.' Now she looked solemn as an owl. 'And just between the two of us, I thought I belonged to a permissive generation but I tell you Brigadier this book is going to be sensational. Cabinet ministers, the lot, talk about indiscretions!'

He was really huffing and puffing by now and she said, 'Would you mind if I sat the rest of this out? I've been dancing all night and my head's starting to spin.'

He jumped at the chance to guide her off the floor and she watched him hurry away, and wondered who he was off to discuss the exposé with, the sisters or their ageing beaux, and shook with silent laughter.

'What's the joke?' Kevin was back beside her.

'I've just set the cat among the pigeons. Let's finish the waltz.' She wound her arms around him and put her head on his shoulder as they danced to the dreamy strains. That way she could almost blot out her surroundings.

'I love you,' Kevin breathed hotly against her cheek, and she thought, No you don't, and you are lucky because loving can tear you to pieces.

'Do you love me?' he was whispering, and as the last notes of the waltz died away the air was filled with the sound of the pipes, and a piper in full magnificent regalia came down the stairs from the minstrels' gallery. He circled the ballroom with measured tread and Kevin muttered, 'What a caterwauling.'

Morag hissed, 'You'll get a dirk in you if anyone hears that.'

The old year was dying and this strange thrilling music was its requiem. They linked crossed hands and sang' 'Should auld acquaintance be forgot,' snaking around the ballroom. Then the first stroke of Big Ben chimed over the loudspeakers and everyone was still, listening, counting silently to twelve.

On the final stroke the piper stepped out again, playing a jubilant air, and the ballroom exploded with elation greeting the new year.

Morag had seen Callum and Rosalie, together in the chain, hands linked. In the first moment of the new year they turned to each other and kissed and jealousy tied tight knots inside her. Hugs and kisses were being bestowed indiscriminately. Morag had been kissed by Kevin, who had whooped, 'Happy new year, baby,' and as she stood there strangers flung arms around her, although Kevin kept hold of her hand.

She backed through the milling crowd through the open door of the dining room, which was empty except for three waitresses. 'Happy new year,' said Morag. 'Happy new year,' they chorused.

The buffet had been appreciated. All the dishes had been well sampled but there was still food remaining, and Morag took a plate and Kevin stared, watching her scoop all that was left of the cold beef wellington and pick up a knife and fork.

'Just going to wish two of my friends a happy new year,' she told him. After the crowded ballroom the rest of the castle was eerily empty. All the lights were on but everyone seemed to have been drawn to the ballroom, and by the time Morag reached the kitchens even the noise and the music were faint. Kevin was with her. As they walked along he asked her where she was going and she said, 'There's no need for you to come, they're not your friends.'

He laughed, and said, 'You're tight.'

'Right,' she'd said. But I won't be tomorrow and what shall I do then?

'Of course,' he said, as she opened the brewhouse door and he saw the two dogs lying on a rug in front of a stove. He still couldn't tell them apart and he hovered in the open doorway.

'Come in if you're coming,' said Morag. 'I'm not to

let Hyde loose. If he's in one of his moods he could
soon clear the ballroom.'

And don't think I'd mind seeing him do it, she
thought. 'Happy new year my old mates,' she said, 'I've
brought you something special for your supper.'

They had already had their supper, there were two
empty bowls to show, but she chopped up the tender
fillet steak and the melt-in-the-mouth pastry, picked up
the bowls and divided it. While they gobbled she said,
'Aren't they beautiful?'

'Handsome,' Kevin agreed, watching warily. 'Can we
leave them now?'

Two great tongues went round two dishes in a final
slurp, and two great heads were raised. I'll let them out
for a couple of minutes first, Morag decided. A second
door in the brewhouse led into an enclosed courtyard,
and she pulled back bars and opened the door. The
dogs went without much enthusiasm.

The cold was like a curtain of ice, flowing into the
heated room. You felt that the air would crackle if you
pushed it aside, but she walked out after the animals
and Kevin followed her a couple of steps before he
stopped, spluttering through chattering teeth, 'I've
never known cold like it.'

There was still no wind, just bitter bitter cold as
though the ice age had come. Kevin backed into the
castle but Morag walked after the dogs, who were
padding morosely towards a log pile against the far
corner.

It hurt to breathe and her eyes were stinging. She
thought crazily, I could go on walking out on to the
cliff top and freeze up all the tears in me. Right now
that doesn't seem a bad idea. Captain Oates saved
himself a lot of pain.

The dogs paused briefly at the wood pile and came
loping back. Mrs Fraser shouted, 'Morag, whatever are
you doing?'

Mrs Fraser was standing with Kevin in the doorway and Morag came back, which she would have done of course, nobody needed to call her although Mrs Fraser began scolding, 'You ought to have more sense than going out on a night like this, dressed as you are. You could get your death of cold out there.'

I could get my death of cold in here, thought Morag. Cold of the heart is what I'm suffering from. She said, 'I was only out for a minute. Anything I can do?'

'Get to bed,' said Kevin, and Mrs Fraser's mouth pursed slightly, although she gave a small nod of agreement.

Kevin was with her still right up to her room, when she stepped inside and almost closed the door leaving him out in the passage. 'No,' she said through the gap, and his face went blank.

'*No?* What do you mean, *no* . . .?'

'N.O.,' she said. 'Good night.'

Astonishment turned ugly, as eyes and lips narrowed. 'I won't ask you again,' he shouted and she closed the door and locked it.

She felt bad about Kevin. Tonight he had been sure he would be sleeping with her and maybe that would have got her through the night, but suppose between sleeping and waking she had sobbed another man's name? Besides she couldn't.

All night Morag had been lacerated with jealousy, but she knew now that until midnight she had had a faint hope that Callum would at least come across and *speak* to her. After all they shared secrets, and briefly, once, they had been lovers. But Callum had not had a moment to spare for Morag, and yet she could not contemplate lying in another man's arms. Although she was sorry for Kevin she was sorrier for herself, because he would soon find somebody else but she had a bleak foreboding bordering on certainty, that she never would.

She started to get out of her dress. Her fingers were still white-tipped from the cold of the courtyard as she fumbled with minute hooks. She wanted if *off*. She hated the dress, and everything connected with the New Year's Eve Ball. She gripped the collar and yanked, ripping the fine material, until she could drag the dress over her head and drop it in a heap on the floor.

In bed she thought, I didn't make a real spectacle of myself. Nobody knows how I feel about Callum. And she remembered the brigadier and wondered if the sisters were assuring him that Morag was no journalist and if he was believing them. She smiled in the darkness but she wept in her sleep . . .

It was still dark when she woke. She raised herself on an elbow and looked at her little bedside clock, the luminous fingers said ten to seven. Her head was clear, and she felt calm with a queer kind of hollow ache.

There would be plenty to do today. Not many of the guests would have left last night, they would want breakfast and Mrs Fraser's small army of helpers would be scurrying around. Morag had not been hired to wait on anyone but the sisters, and anyhow she had practically handed in her notice, but she needed something to keep her occupied until she could get away.

A deep stillness seemed to have settled, and when she went to the window it was as though nothing moved all over the island. She knew that was an illusion. Not many New Year's Eve ceilidhs would have finished yet, but up here there wasn't a sound. It was cold, Lord it was cold. She put on a thick sweater and skirt, and thick tights under her boots, and spent a while putting some colour on her face.

The corridor outside her room was empty, although for the first time since Morag came here all the rooms behind those closed doors were in use. A little farther along were the sisters, probably sleeping, it was much too early to disturb them. There was Kevin's room and she wasn't going near that. She went to Callum's door.

'Tea or coffee?' she could say if he was awake.

She opened the door a little, quietly and slowly, and the light from the passage showed a smooth unrumpled bed and she shut the door again. Rosalie could have been in there and what would she have said then? 'Tea or coffee sir and madam?' That had been a mad thing to do but her need to see Callum in his own bed, alone, had overridden everything.

Well he wasn't. The music would have stopped but downstairs guests could still be filling drawing rooms, he might still be hosting the party. If he wasn't all she had learned by opening his door was that if Callum was in any bed, it wasn't his own.

She had to stop this. It was stupid and useless. But she had never before known such despair, as though losing one man could mean that the rest of her life would be a disaster.

All the activity was downstairs. The guests had gone, either on their way or to their bedrooms, and that included Rosalie and Callum, because neither of them was helping Mrs Fraser and her helpers. Morag ran the dogs around the courtyard. She would exercise them later but it was still dark now, so she fed them and joined the cleaners, who were moving doggedly and silently through the great empty rooms, sweeping all traces of the ball before them.

The buffet in the dining room was being replaced by a breakfast buffet, and Morag kept well in the background. She didn't want to get caught up by the morning-after guests. At nine o'clock she looked in the sisters' room, but Polly was the only one to open eyes. The sisters were deep in slumber. Their dresses were thrown over chairs, the rest of their clothes strewn around, as it must have been after the balls and the parties of their youth. Even the jewellery was in glittering disarray on the dressing table. Morag could imagine them chattering and giggling as they got out of their finery. Once it would have been about their own lovers. Last night they would relive how Callum had looked at Rosalie, what he might have said to her. Last night's big romance for them had been Callum and Rosalie.

She tidied quietly, replacing the jewellery in boxes that would go into the wall safe, hanging up dresses. But neither sleeper stirred and even Polly settled back, nose between paws, on the bottom of Flora's bed.

Then she went to make her own bed and was horrified when she picked up the dress to see that she really had ripped it. It might be mended if she stitched close to the seams, and she could hardly leave it in this state.

She took it downstairs to the sewing room where there was matching cotton still in the machine from when she was altering the dress to fit. First she had to tack it together and she was starting to do that when Callum walked in.

He was wearing dark slacks, and dark roll neck sweater under a black leather jacket. He was shaved and clear eyed, and he made her jump so that the needle jabbed her finger and she yelped, 'Ouch'.

'Rough night?' he inquired pleasantly, eyeing the ripped dress. She took her finger out of her mouth and watched a tiny welling of blood and said, through gritted teeth,

'Lovely thank you. Did you enjoy yourself?'

'Very much.' He sat down on the end of the sewing table, arms crossed, looking down at her. 'What's this about you being a journalist?'

She had expected some reaction to that and this morning she wasn't sure it had been such a good idea to say it at all. She went back to sucking her finger, she couldn't sew until he had gone and mumbled, 'How do you know I'm not?'

'It wouldn't surprise me.' He knew she had had a

variety of jobs, she could have done a little freelance journalism as well. 'Did you tell the brigadier that the memoirs are going to be the hottest property since Lady Chatterley?'

That was more or less her drift. In fact it was exactly what she had told him. 'Er—sort of,' she said.

'Because I've just had a deputation of anxious old men to see if I can stop publication,' said Callum, and she bit her lip on an hysterical urge to giggle.

'Dear, oh dear,' she muttered.

'I presume it was a joke.'

She had pretended to Kevin it was a joke, but she had said it because she had hated the fat little man who was telling her that Callum's engagement to Rosalie would be announced any time. 'Not really,' she said.

Dark eyebrows rose as he said quietly, 'You're not seriously considering trying to get those old letters published? If you are let me remind you that they are not your property, and secondly that nobody is going to give a damn about them except the old codgers who wrote them and maybe their families.'

'I know that.'

'Then what's it all about?'

'I'll tell you what it's all about. The brigadier reminded me that most of your guests think I'm your mistress.'

'And we mustn't have that.' He wasn't thinking of her. He wanted Rosalie reassured that Morag was no part of his past or present.

'Too ruddy true,' she said. 'And I didn't feel like telling the pompous prig that I'm here because my brother's a crook so I said I was a journalist.'

'Sounds slightly more respectable,' said Callum.

'So if you decide to tell them I'm not will you also make it clear that I'm not an easy lady either.'

It didn't seem incongruous, saying that, it was the truth, but when Callum said, 'I'll stress it,' he began to smile—he had to be remembering the north wing.

She snapped, 'And don't you dare laugh at me.'

'I don't,' he said. 'But you didn't see the deputation.'

She could imagine it, and she was glad that that was amusing him, and her own lips began to twitch in a reluctant smile. 'What are you going to do?'

He shrugged. 'Let it ride. It's a reasonable explanation of why you're here and I think most of them were secretly flattered.' He looked down again at the dress she was holding and said, 'You must have been in a hurry to get out of that.'

He wasn't jealous, he was amused. When she had seen him kiss Rosalie she had felt such pain, and the thought of him making love to Rosalie was something she dare not dwell on. But he could smile, because what Morag did hardly concerned him at all. She remembered his words, 'You could never get to me in a hundred years,' and heard herself say lightly, 'I was. By midnight I'd had enough. How long did the ball go on?'

'About threeish.' In the old days New Year's Eve balls at this castle had seen the night through but the sisters had been younger then.

'It went off very well I thought,' Morag said chattily. 'Most of the guests will be going today won't they? They've got a fair day for it so far, what's the forecast?'

'Not good, I'd better be moving.'

'Are you leaving?' She wanted to try to keep him here and that would be pathetic.

'Flying a few of them out,' he said.

'And then coming back?'

'Yes.'

'Keep an eye on the weather or you could be grounded on the mainland.'

'I'll get back.'

'Rosalie isn't leaving?' And when he smiled and said

her parents were but she wasn't she said, 'She'll be waiting for you?'

'Of course.'

She bit her lip so hard that her teeth nearly cut into the flesh until he left the room, to stop herself demanding savagely,

'Did Rosalie's dress get ripped last night?'

She botched the repair. It was a tricky job, the tear needed a backing to strengthen it. The bodice was fitted and there was not enough spare material to pull together neatly. But after a fashion the dress was mended and she took it back to her room.

Flora had made her a present of it but she would never wear it again, and she would hate to open the wardrobe and see it hanging there like a skeleton in the cupboard, reminding her of the night when her dreams had died.

She heard the helicopter as she walked along the corridor with the sisters' breakfast tray, and when she carried it into the room Flora said happily, 'There goes Callum.'

'He'll be back,' said Dora. They were both sitting up in bed and they beamed at Morag.

'Wasn't it a wonderful ball?' said Flora. 'Did you and Kevin enjoy yourselves?'

'Oh, it was,' said Morag. 'Oh, we did.'

'Rosalie and Callum never left each other's sides,' said Dora. 'They were together all night.' I think they were too, thought Morag.

'He's always been devoted to her although he'd never admit it,' said Flora dreamily, 'but wasn't it just like a story when he saw her last night and realised how much he loved her?'

Morag handed them their lemon juice.

'An Easter wedding,' said Flora ecstatically and Dora smiled. 'If they want to wait that long.'

'Talking of books,' said Morag abruptly, 'I've got a

confession to make.' She had wondered how she was going to explain to the sisters, but now she was thankful to have something to say that might shut them up for a while about Rosalie.

She said, 'You haven't heard, about the memoirs?' They both shook their heads and she went on, 'Well last night I'm afraid I told the brigadier I was a journalist and that I was here to write your book.'

That puzzled them. 'Well you are helping us of course,' said Flora, 'but you're not a journalist are you?'

'No, but he thinks, and most of them think,' she gulped, 'that Callum and I were having an affair before he brought me up here.'

'We wondered ourselves,' said Dora, 'a girl like you leaving London for Calla. But that was before you told us about Kevin.'

'Saying I was a journalist seemed a good explanation at the time,' said Morag, 'but I seem to have given the impression that all sorts of secrets are coming out and I'm sorry if I've embarrassed anybody. Some of them seem worried.'

'They would be.' Flora suddenly looked mischievous and young.

'But we can't have rumours going around about Morag and Callum,' said Dora briskly, 'even if we know they are nonsense. It wouldn't be fair on Rosalie. And I'm sure Kevin wouldn't like it so I think we should say you're writing our book.'

'It might be amusing,' Flora mused, 'to have it published. Privately of course.'

'I don't know about that,' said Dora. 'We'd have to see Callum about it.'

Then they both drank their lemon juice while Morag sorted out their clothes for the day, and tried to close her ears as they relived magical moments at the ball, all of which seemed centred on Callum and Rosalie. She thought wildly, I wonder if they'd be thrilled to hear he didn't sleep in his own bed last night so he and Rosalie probably stayed good and close till morning.

But she couldn't shut her ears or eyes when Rosalie walked in. She would have liked to because Rosalie was glowing with such triumph that she might as well have danced around the room proclaiming, 'I did it, I got him.'

She was wearing a cowl-necked pink suit, fluffy and soft and warm, and grey suede boots, her bright hair curling back from her radiant face. She looked more like Marilyn Monroe than ever this morning as she flew to kiss the sisters, and then kissed Morag as though she was so happy she wanted to hug the whole world.

'What a handsome man,' she gurgled at Morag. 'He's like a Greek god.'

'Callum?' Morag croaked.

'No,' Rosalie fell about laughing. 'Your Kevin. I'm so pleased for you. I think it's lovely you've got him back.'

'Well he——' Morag began, but Rosalie was scooping up Polly and planting a kiss on top of her head. 'You don't need to stay,' she told Morag. 'We can manage. Besides,' she made a cute little grimace, 'I want to talk.'

Morag went out of the room, leaving behind a smiling Rosalie and the two sisters waiting with bated breath. It might be earlier than an Easter wedding, because that had to be what Rosalie wanted to talk about, and Morag stood outside the door, her hands clenched into fists.

Sometime last night Callum had asked Rosalie to marry him. What a lunatic thing for him to do. Morag wanted to scream and bang her fists against the door—couldn't anyone see that there could be no lasting happiness between those two? Rosalie would make him a doll of a wife and he was not the man for dolls. She would never get under the skin, much less reach the depths in him.

I believe I could have done that, Morag thought, walking down the corridor with long fast strides. I think I could have reached him, given time. But he hadn't wanted total commitment, and Rosalie would make the prettiest bride, and a decorative mistress of Calla for the next fifty years.

Guests were leaving in shoals, all of them muffled up now against the cold outside. Most of them had heard, over breakfast, that Morag Macdonald was a journalist; and although some of them thought it an unlikely tale, the news that the sisters were considering telling all was amusing most and disturbing a few.

When Morag was cornered in the hall by an overbearing dowager who glared at her and said, 'Young woman, I hope you know what you're doing,' she stared blankly back. 'This book——' boomed the large lady.

'Oh that! I sometimes wonder if any of us know what we're doing.' Morag said bitterly.

There was plenty she could be doing. She could have found any number of tasks which would help with the smooth running of Calla Castle. Some guests were remaining and she wondered if the sisters would be able to resist making the announcement before Callum returned.

Morag turned in the hall and went back to her room and wrapped herself in several more layers of clothing, topping them with a greatcoat. In the kitchens she told Mrs Fraser, 'I'm taking the dogs for a run.'

'Don't go too far,' warned Hamish. 'It's going to break.'

He meant the respite they were getting from the gale force winds, and Morag made herself smile and say, 'Not till the guests get home I hope.'

She put on a woollen hat, pulled up her coat collar and scarf around her face, dug her gloved hands deep into her pockets and walked for miles. She could have gone visiting. New Year's Day would be open house all over Calla.

But you were never sure sbout Hyde and the islanders thought Morag Macdonald was Callum's woman and she could take neither digs nor disapproval today.

So she kept clear of the harbour and skirted the crofts, and walked through the heather and the rough grasses, round the ice-edged lochs. As the dogs ran at full stretch covering three miles to her one, she walked the land of her childhood saying goodbye to it all because when she left Calla this time she would never return again.

It was a cold and lonely goodbye as she circled the island and came once more to the cottage where she was born. Last time she had stopped, looked at door and windows at the front, all boarded up, and gone away. Now she went round the back but there was no sign of the little yard, nor the seaweed bed where her father and mother had grown vegetables. Weeds and grass had covered everything, but the back door had crumbled away and she stepped into what had been the kitchen.

It had been a cosy cottage, kept neat as a pin by her mother. There had been handmade rugs on the floor and a dresser with willow pattern cups and saucers and plates. Mary Macdonald had sold or given away everything before she and Morag left Calla, and the cottage had probably stood empty ever since.

It was hard to believe it had ever been a home. Plaster and paper had peeled off damp-stained walls and the flagstoned floor was carpeted with moss, crisp with hoar frost. The front room was the living room, where a peat fire had burned. There was no door now and grey light filtered in from the kitchen as Morag walked through the gap between the two rooms and heard the dogs snuffling behind her.

She would always remember waiting in here for her father to come home, while the storm raged and hope died. She had stood close by the window, her face pressed to it, all through that night, and she went to the window now and through a space between the boarding she saw that it was starting to snow again.

Everyone who wanted to leave Calla today should have been safely clear by now, but she had a tough climb ahead up to the castle and she mustn't leave it a minute longer. She had been out all day, and now the snow was coming again and she had better move fast.

She could have gone down into the village round the harbour and found shelter there, and there were other whitewashed cottages dotted along the winding rising road, but if she didn't return to the castle it might start a panic. One way or another she had caused trouble enough.

She whistled to the dogs. But even they were flagging before they reached the lodge. Morag had gone at such a frantic pace that she was sweating although it was snowing. She had half run half stumbled all the way, and she almost stopped at the lodge. The snow was thickening all the time, but the drive up to the castle was only a few more hundred yards and she had just about enough strength left to make it, round to one of the side doors.

It was as though winter had taken a breather long enough for the sisters to hold their ball. Now it was stirring again with a vengeance. The wind was coming up, the snow was coming down, and Morag leaned against the wall in the passage, while the dogs padded wearily towards the smell of food in the kitchens.

They brought a querulous Mrs Fraser. 'We were thinking of sending a search party out for you. I suppose you've been calling on half the village?'

Morag said, 'Sorry, I didn't notice how time was passing. Anything interesting happen while I've been out?'

'Nothing anyone's told me about,' said Mrs Fraser. So nobody was actually arranging the wedding yet. 'Now you *are* back,' she said, 'you'd better get out of those clothes and give me a hand with their dinner.'

'Sure,' said Morag. Now there was no need to keep moving she could have slid down the wall from weariness, and Mrs Fraser said suddenly, 'Well perhaps not tonight, you look all in.'

Morag took the back stairs up to her room and a while to make herself presentable. She would have liked to crawl into bed but she had to get down there and find out what was happening, and if anyone but the Frasers had been concerned about her, nobody came to check that she was all right.

The large drawing room was still in use, and Morag walked into what was still a party atmosphere. Someone was playing the piano, there was talk and laughter, nearly everyone seemed to have a drink.

Rosalie sat with the sisters and Kevin sat opposite. He had a sketch pad and he was sketching. Dora saw Morag first and said, 'Here's Morag,' and then Flora and Rosalie looked down the room towards her, but Kevin kept his head bowed over his work.

'You've been calling on friends?' questioned Flora when Morag reached them.

Morag said 'Yes' because she had been saying goodbye to ghosts.

Kevin drew another stroke, he was sketching Rosalie, and when he finally glanced up at Morag she knew she was not forgiven for last night.

Dora explained, 'Kevin is going to paint Rosalie with us.' Their portrait was almost finished but Morag supposed Rosalie's beautiful young face could be fitted in somewhere to make a trio and a real family portrait.

'A surprise for Callum,' Flora whispered. 'Don't breathe a word.'

Kevin was sitting here, openly sketching, so it was hardly a secret.

Morag asked, 'Doesn't he know?'

Rosalie said, 'He's not back yet.'

Alarm bells rang in Morag's head. 'But he won't be flying in this.' They didn't know what she was talking about. Kevin ignored her and the sisters and Rosalie simply looked puzzled. 'What?' said Rosalie.

The fires were burning and the chandeliers were glittering. Heavy green velvet drapes were drawn across all the windows, and there was enough noise to drown the rising wind. They were insulated in this elegant room and they hadn't a clue what was happening outside.

Morag pulled the hanging sash by the nearest window and the curtains swished back and the window was white with snow that was snatched away as soon as it settled in a mad churning dance.

Silence spread through the room. The pianist stopped playing, more curtains were opened and now you could hear the wind. Dora put a hand over Flora's hand and said quietly, 'He won't try to get back in this.'

'Oh yes he will,' Rosalie contradicted gaily. 'He promised me.'

Morag turned back to the window, staring out into the whiteness and the blackness beyond. She daren't let herself think about the helicopter, more fragile than her father's boat, caught up in the storm. She pulled the sash again to close the curtains, and now all the guests were talking about the change in the weather and whether they would be cut off on Calla, what they would do if they were.

They had known the risks, it wouldn't be the first winter this had happened, and so long as it only lasted a few days most of them would face it with equanimity. One man went to 'phone, and came back to report that the line was dead.

A shadow had fallen across the sisters. Their faces looked pinched and old and Morag comforted them. 'He won't try.'

'Oh yes he will,' laughed Rosalie, and Morag could have shaken her.

Everybody began reassuring each other, and the sisters, that Callum was too experienced a pilot to risk flying in weather like this, but all the time Rosalie kept insisting that he would be back. She looked so incredibly seductive, smiling a smug little smile, that Morag knew that some of them had to be thinking that he could be besotted enough to try to get back to her at any price. She was like a siren, combing her hair and singing her song, and the rocks and the dark waters waiting.

'This painting,' said Morag, 'where exactly are you going to put Rosalie?' and then Kevin had to tell her and the sisters listened, and then Morag told them that she had walked the island today and gone to her old cottage. She had worn the dogs out, even Hyde was so exhausted he was almost amiable.

'You must be exhausted yourself,' exclaimed Flora.

'I think I'm sleepwalking,' Morag admitted and laughed, and felt that she would never sleep again until they knew for sure that Callum was safe. And if he was not . . .

She couldn't think of that. It was not possible. If he had crashed into the sea all the lights around her would have gone out and her heart would have stopped. If she was still alive and breathing so was he, and she stayed by the sisters and talked of other things.

They were trying to hide their anxiety, each concerned for the other, and Morag thought—if this room would empty I would put my arms around you like the women in the cottage put their arms around my mother. But no one held and comforted the sisters and maybe it was better this way, pretending they were not afraid.

Dinner was served in the great dining room, where there were no curtains at the windows to hide the swirling snow. Morag helped, carrying dishes, serving. She could no more have sat down and eaten than she could have flown from the battlements. Below stairs everyone was grim faced although Hamish was adamant that Callum would not have left the mainland. 'Of *course* he wouldn't,' Morag kept saying.

There was his chair, as always, at the head of the table, and Rosalie, blithe as a bird, sitting between the sisters. She wasn't acting, as they were. Rosalie had no doubts and no fears, because Rosalie always got what she wanted, and she had Callum and nothing would keep him away from her. So she ate her meal and chattered charmingly, as if she was already mistress of the castle with Callum's ring on her finger.

Morag fetched and carried, moving like an automaton. Unless she kept busy she would find herself, face pressed against a window, staring out blindly, like that last vigil that had ended in heartbreak.

She was stacking plates and cutlery very carefully, into a dumb waiter in a cupboard of a room leading off the dining room, when the buzz of talk ceased abruptly, and almost at once Rosalie said into the silence, '*Callum . . .*'

He had just come in to the room. He couldn't have been much wetter if he had come out of the sea. There were snow flakes in his black hair, and Morag stood in the doorway of the little room, unable to speak or move.

Everyone else was moving. The guests down the long table were carrying on as if he had won gold at the Olympics, something very like a cheer went up. Flora and Dora reached for each other, now they could admit they had been rather concerned, and Rosalie jumped out of her seat and flung her arms around his neck.

'I knew you were coming,' she told him.

'She has such faith in you,' said Flora wonderingly. 'She believes you can do anything.' Morag thought— that's not faith, that's being too stupid to see danger.

But Rosalie had been right, Callum had not been able to keep away and Morag came out of her state of shock at the relief of seeing him alive and started to feel sick.

Her unsmiling face must have been conspicuous among all the beaming ones because he said, 'Did you think I'd be coming back?' and down the length of the room he was talking to her.

She jerked her head towards a window. 'I think you were a bloody fool to risk coming through this.'

That struck a discordant note. Rosalie squeaked a shocked protest, and this company would certainly consider that Morag Macdonald should not be swearing at the master of Calla.

'Aren't we all at times?' said Callum, and he was no bigger fool than she was, going through hell because he might never reach here.

He was here now and Rosalie was cuddling up against him like a kitten, and Morag made herself turn back to the dumb waiter, emotions churning in her. Relief, jealousy, anger—at herself, at him. Lust—if she had not turned away she might have gone into the dining room, and started brushing the snowflakes out of his hair just to touch him.

She got away as quickly and as quietly as she could, and went to her own room. She could take no more today. She had to be tired. She dreamt that she was back in the old cottage, standing at the window looking out into the storm, waiting for someone who would never come . . .

CHAPTER EIGHT

NEXT morning there was less talk in the kitchens about the fourteen unexpected guests who were here for nobody knew how long, than about Callum Maconnell's crash landing last night. As soon as she walked in Morag heard all about that. The helicopter had been blown off course and come down along the coast, a few yards from the cottage of a crofter who had a van. The van had almost made it to the castle.

And nobody seemed surprised that Callum had arrived here in one piece. There were half a dozen helpers who had been marooned in the castle, and Morag's outburst had been repeated and Jimmy MacTavish, who was at the kitchen table with a large bowl of porridge, agreed that the master had been a 'bloody fool'. But he grinned as he added, 'Och, the black Maconnells always have the divil's own luck.'

There would be no getting off Calla, nor even out of the castle, today. When Morag opened the door into the courtyard she was confronted by a blizzard and the dogs ventured out very briefly indeed. It was blinding, and blowing so hard that you could hardly stand up in it let alone make any progress.

Some of the guests were already gathered in the dining room, helping themselves to breakfast and watching the white whirlwind outside the windows. There was a general feeling of excitement, and they were chattering happily when Morag went in.

Rosalie was not there, and neither was Callum. Kevin was tucking in to scrambled eggs and bacon at the end of the long dining table, and Morag poured herself coffee and took a bowl of muesli and hot milk and after a

166

moment's hesitation sat down beside him. 'Hello,' she said.

But Kevin was still deeply offended. He looked up at a window and demanded curtly, 'How long are we going to get stuck here?'

'I don't know.' Mischievously she added, 'I think the record was three months,' and immediately wished she hadn't, because everybody gasped with dismay, and she quickly said, 'I'm joking.' She wasn't, but she couldn't remember that winter, it was history. 'A day or two maybe,' she said, although it could easily be a week or two, and turned to Kevin. 'You'll need that for your painting.'

He finished his breakfast without exchanging another word with her, eating fast to show that he was anxious to get away, and when he stood up he said, 'You know where to find me if you want me.'

The schoolroom-cum-studio she supposed, and could think of no way in which she was likely to want Kevin.

The sisters were delighted at the turn in the weather. Most of the remaining guests had intended leaving Calla today, only a few of their oldest friends were staying the week out. Now they had a mixed bag, and the prospect of a lively time. They were planning a fancy dress party for tonight when Morag took in their breakfast tray.

She walked back towards the main staircase and near the top of the stairs she saw Callum. She supposed a time must come when that would not be like a blow to the heart, but this morning her first sight of his tall dark figure stopped her dead in her tracks.

A woman and a man were with him, the man grizzled and distinguished, the woman slim and blonde and well preserved, and the woman was saying gaily, 'Nothing scares you does it? Nothing stops you getting where you want to be,' and both the woman and the man laughed. The woman shook her head in mock reproach and they went on down the stairs.

Morag walked slowly but Callum had turned as though he was waiting for her, and when she reached him he asked, 'How's your mood this morning?'

'I still think you were crazy.' He could have come down in the sea as easily as on land, even the devil's luck runs out sometime, and she mimicked, '"Nothing stops you getting where you want to be. Nothing scares you," I don't know why everyone thinks that's so almighty clever, you could say that about a bull in a china shop.'

There was nothing bullish about Callum, he was more your black leopard, and every time she thought of the danger he had put himself in she felt angry and helpless. He said, 'Who says I wasn't scared?'

'I hope you were, because some of your womenfolk don't think you're indestructible. Flora and Dora looked a hundred years old last night,' she snapped back.

'How do they look this morning?' This morning of course was a different story and she had to admit.

'Fifty years younger.' And she couldn't help smiling. 'They've got all these guests who can't get away. What *are* you going to do with them?'

He shrugged. 'Personally very little. But it'll be like old times for them. A houseparty at the castle.'

'Were houseparties fun?' There were people in the hall below, doors were open and there was a fair amount of movement, but up here for the moment there was only Morag and Callum.

'They bored me out of my mind,' he said.

She wished she could say, 'You still have your secret pad,' but she couldn't, and she watched Tom Corbishley, the Canadian business man, replace the 'phone in the alcove and stride away looking disgruntled. The lines would stay out of order so long as the gales blew and she quipped, 'How many businesses will grind to a halt if your tycoons are stuck here for the winter?'

'We don't have that many tycoons trapped,' said Callum.

'Well there's you for a start. I hope you can trust all your managers to manage in your absence.' She was just babbling but as soon as she said it she realised that that was a dumb remark from Alistair's sister.

'A very loyal bunch are my management.' He smiled, but there was a quiet grimness in his voice, and she believed him. Alistair for one would never risk cheating Callum again. Callum scared Alistair half to death.

He can scare me too, thought Morag. They stood side by side, both leaning on the carved oak balustrade and looking down into the hall, not touching although she could feel the pull between them as if she had wandered into a magnetic field. She would leave here, he might marry Rosalie, but whenever and if ever they met again Morag would always be able to disturb him a little. And, God knows, he disturbed her.

'You need not be bored,' he said. 'You can always get on with the memoirs. You did tell me you could write a book.'

'I never did.' Then she remembered, in Alistair's apartment when Callum had commented on her varied careers. 'That was just talk, as well you know.'

'Well, I think you could. They now have ambitions to publish privately.'

'Will you let them?'

'Suppose you pull it together and then we'll see.'

When the idea was put to her straight it sounded almost feasible. She had been typing out their reminiscences and there was a mine of copy and information among their souvenirs. She would enjoy getting it together, much more than she would enjoy watching Rosalie playing the hostess of Calla Castle with the sisters, or listening to everyone saying that Callum and Rosalie were made for each other.

'You could use my office,' Callum offered and that

clinched it. She would be cut off from all of them in there. 'You've a good team of lawyers of course for if we get sued,' she said.

From down below Rosalie trilled, 'So there you are,' and came running up the stairs. As she came she called, 'We're having a fancy dress party tonight. Do you know what Lydia Moreton's just said? She says it's like being on a luxury cruise and you're the captain.'

'Hi, skipper,' murmured Morag.

'Keep an eye open for icebergs,' said Callum. 'I name this liner the *Titanic*.'

Morag was grinning when Rosalie reached them and got a sharp glint from baby-blue eyes, although Rosalie immediately smiled. 'Won't a fancy dress party be a scream? We'll have to make-do but there are lots of old clothes.' She dimpled. 'And the men could always wear some of the armour.' And Morag had a vision of figures clanking around in ancient hardwear and toppling over like ninepins.

'Morag, you can sew can't you?' Rosalie had heard why Morag's mother came to the castle, and improvising costumes meant getting someone to make them fit.

'Sorry,' Morag said hastily, 'I've got a book to write.'

She wasn't being given Callum's desk, but he had a writing bureau brought in for her. One of the matching pair from the small drawing room, which contained the letters and the photographs, and her notes and typing. There was an electronic typewriter on his desk, but he didn't offer her that either.

While the bureau was being shifted Hyde had joined the procession baring his teeth, and now he lay on the Indian rug still rumbling and Callum said, 'He'd better stay.'

'You should be quite cosy,' said Rosalie.

She was happy to be leaving Morag shut in here, busy and bothering nobody; and Morag wondered if

Callum was too. The sisters wanted their book ghosted, he was probably humouring them as he usually did. But this was a good way of getting rid of two disruptive elements, Morag and Hyde. 'All right?' he said now.

'Yes thank you,' said Morag. 'We'll both be very comfortable.'

She watched Callum and Rosalie walking away from her down the length of the library. Rosalie was speaking softly and smiling up at Callum, and Morag was not listening although she couldn't take her eyes off them. At the far end just before they walked into the corridor, Callum put an arm around Rosalie, and that seemed so protective and so intimate that Morag felt like someone peering through a bedroom keyhole.

She closed her door and stood for a little while by the window, looking out into the snow. She was no part of the family, nor the guests, and she was not even needed as staff now. She almost believed that she could stay in this room for days and nobody would miss her not being around the castle. She sat down at the bureau and began to sort out the mass of material before her.

The sisters were her first callers while Morag was still trying to get some order into all this. So far it had usually been Flora, who dipped into their keepsakes haphazardly and then started talking around whatever she came up with.

Dora had not been far behind. Dora had enjoyed reliving memories, but now there was a prospect of the memoirs reaching a wider public some of Dora's early misgivings had been revived. The sisters looked at the photographs and writings that Morag had placed on the top of Callum's desk and Dora said, 'You will use your discretion won't you?'

'Of course,' said Morag. 'And I shall leave everything here so it will be entirely up to you what you do with it.'

That seemed to reassure Dora. She picked up the

photograph of a young army officer, looking very slim and dapper, and smiled. 'Dear Leonard, he's hardly changed at all.'

My stars, thought Morag, I do believe it's the brigadier! 'What times we had,' mused Dora softly, still smiling.

'Such happy times,' said Flora, smiling too. 'And now Callum and Rosalie are giving us another love story.'

'Rosalie was telling me you're planning a fancy dress party for tonight,' Morag said quickly.

She could not let them go on about Callum and Rosalie. It was like a superstition, a taboo, don't let anyone tell you anything and nothing too dreadful will happen.

Flora brightened even more. 'Dora's going as Queen Victoria in black satin and jet jewellery, and I'm the Snow Queen in white and pearls.'

'What a good idea,' said Morag. 'Shall you need me?'

They looked at each other. 'To help us dress?' said Flora. 'Oh we can manage,' said Dora. There were plenty of staff and friends around at the moment. 'What shall you be?' Dora went on. 'You must come and choose something to wear. There are trunks of old clothes, old uniforms, some of our dresses. The drawing room looks like a jumble sale, and you're so clever you're sure to come up with something really ingenious.'

Flora said, 'Rosalie's going to wear the little blue chiffon dress, it must be over fifty years old, it's a wonder it hasn't fallen to pieces. She's wearing a bandeau round her head and long strings of beads.' Flora dimpled like a girl. 'They used to call us the Bright Young Things, I used to break hearts when I wore that dress, and you can't imagine how pretty Rosalie looks in it.'

Oh but I can thought Morag. Like Marilyn Monroe

in *Gentlemen Prefer Blondes* and I can't think of any fancy dress that would make me equal to that, so I think I shall keep away.

'One little problem,' said Dora, before they left. 'Some of them only expected to be staying overnight, they only brought one change. We're getting together what we can, would you have anything you could spare?'

Morag brought down what she felt she could manage without, amused at the thought of dowagers and debs in her hand-me-downs. She wondered if the Frasers had been called on to contribute and the mind boggled.

After the sisters had gone she expected to be left alone, but in fact she had a steady stream of callers wanting to discuss the book. Callum had been right when he said that the ones who expected to be mentioned were secretly flattered, because they all ended up talking, and Morag was amused and entertained and taking notes by the page.

Around lunchtime she went down to the kitchens. Hyde had been so well behaved that her callers had all presumed he was Jekyll, but by midday he began to get restive, and she closed the bureau on all the papers, and stuck a 'Gone to Lunch' note in her typewriter.

She fed both dogs in the brewhouse, and sat down at the kitchen table with a bowl of the meat and vegetable soup that was being provided for the staff. Maggie MacTavish, who had dished out the soup, asked her, 'Is it a fact you're here to write a book about them?'

'Yes,' said Morag.

'And here we were all thinking you were . . .' Maggie didn't finish that. As Morag finished her soup she said, 'Miss Rosalie'll make a bonny wee bride.'

'Aye,' said Morag. 'Real bonny.'

She took the two dogs to the door leading from the brewhouse to the little courtyard. 'Out,' she said, and the dogs slunk into the whirling whiteness like two black shadows being swallowed up almost at once. After a couple of minutes she called but there was no sign of them. Snow-filled air was rushing in, if anybody walked in here they were going to bellow at her to shut the door but she couldn't do that leaving the animals out there. She shouted their names but the wind snatched her voice away, and she stepped outside. They couldn't be far, unless the gate was open, this was a small enclosure.

She kept her head down, her arm up shielding her face, and stumbled around, peering and shouting for them. The ground was slippery as a skating rink, the air was thick with snow, and in spite of the high walls the winds were strong enough to batter her like a punch ball.

She was swept off her feet when she was almost across the courtyard, partly by the wind and mainly by the dogs who were rushing around in a crazy game. They had both had a boring morning, they were working off surplus energy and they sent her spinning against the woodpile, which was frozen so hard that not a log stirred.

If she hadn't been numb with cold it would probably have hurt more, but it gave her a nasty jar and she cursed them both as she got groggily up. They went back with her, shaking themselves vigorously as soon as they were indoors, while she slumped down on to the long stone slab that ran the length of the wall.

When Callum walked into the brewhouse from the kitchens she was still gasping for breath and he said, 'Don't tell me you've been outside.'

The dogs were dripping wet and so was she. 'All right,' she panted. 'I won't.' She stood up and winced and he said, 'What have you done to yourself now?'

'I fell into the woodpile.'

'What were you doing at the woodpile?'

'I let the dogs out and they didn't come back. I thought maybe the gate was open so I went to get them and what with it blowing a gale and them being snow crazy I got knocked into the woodpile.' Now her teeth were starting to chatter. 'Oh boy, it's cold outside. Were you looking for me?'

'I was,' he said. 'If you get bored with the memoirs several of them are prepared to pay well for a temporary secretary.'

She was not getting bored. She was getting involved. 'I'm not bored,' she said. 'I'm hearing some fascinating stuff. But I suppose I could take notes and type for an hour or two, so long as it's understood that I'm not exactly tycoon standard.'

'That's very obliging of you,' said Callum.

She replied, 'We aim to please,' because her tongue ran away when she was talking to him and she said the daftest things.

'You'd better get into a hot bath,' he said.

'Is the heating going to hold out? Is the food going to hold out?'

'Yes.'

'That's all right then. And now you've arranged secretarial services for the workers, and there's a fancy dress do for the party goers tonight. Queen Victoria and the Snow Queen no less.' She couldn't bring herself to say, 'And Rosalie as a bright young thing.' 'What are you going as?' she asked.

They had walked out of the brewhouse, and through the kitchens. 'What do you suggest?' he said.

She longed to slip her arm through his, but she kept her hands by her sides and said gaily, 'You could wear an eyepatch and be a pirate like the black Maconnell.' Nobody knew what she was feeling.

'I don't think I'll bother. Get out of those wet clothes.'

'That sounds a rather improper suggestion.' She laughed, and so did he as they parted and she went up the stairs to her room.

The first thing she saw when she walked in was her portrait propped up beside the bed. Returned by Kevin obviously, who no longer felt that he needed it around. She didn't much need it herself. She pushed it under the bed and went into the bathroom.

By the time she had taken a hot bath she was discovering tender spots where she had hit the logpile. Even through the thickness of her clothes it had made a hard and jagged impact and she could have done without the discomfort. This was the second time the dogs had sent her flying. Coming back to Calla hadn't done her much good. She had the bruises to show, and others that did not show. An aching loneliness and longing she would carry all her life.

Apart from Hyde, stretched out on the rug, the office was empty when she returned to it and she said, 'You've got your nerve after what you did. Thanks to you I'm hobbling around.' That was an exaggeration but she put a cushion on her chair before she got on with her work.

There were newspaper and magazine accounts, letters and photographs covering the sisters' wedding to the Maconnell brothers, and Morag immersed herself in that day. That was when Flora came to Calla Castle, when this story began, but if the book was ending with the wedding of Callum and Rosalie, somebody else would have to write about it.

She saw Callum again during the afternoon. He brought Tom Corbishley with him and the grey-haired Canadian explained that he was drafting some ideas on sales promotion to be put in front of a conference next month, could Morag type them out for him?

'I should think so,' she said, and for that she was allowed to sit at Callum's desk and use the electronic typewriter. For that an audio-machine was produced, which meant that her not-too-hot shorthand was not needed. Tom would dictate into a note-taker and then bring her the tapes. 'I'll do them this evening,' she said.

She worked late. She heard the music and the voices as she came out of the office into the library but she didn't follow them, not even to look in and see what spectacles the guests were making of themselves.

The kitchens were empty. There was no sign of Jekyll so she fed Hyde and let him out and told him, 'If you don't come back you're on your own.' But he did and as she was about to shut the brewhouse door on him she looked back and smiled wryly. 'We're two of a pair. We should stick together. Come on.'

She went with the dog up the back stairs and that night he slept on the rug in her room . . .

She had no chores now. Next morning the sisters' tray was taken up with several others and innumerable cups of tea and coffee. The Frasers had had practice in organising a routine for the comfort of guests and everything was running smoothly. For five days nobody set foot outside the castle, except the dogs in the courtyard. The snow never stopped and the winds raged, but inside it was like being in a good hotel. The billiards room was open, bridge foursomes developed. Meals were served with a great deal of silverware and crystal glasses and some very good wine from the castle cellars, and every evening there was music and dancing.

Morag kept clear of the social scene. She had no desire to join in and nobody urged her. The sisters looked into the office every day and they were all for her concentrating on the memoirs, because she was only here as long as Calla was cut off. She might not take the first boat out but she was getting away as soon as she could.

They talked for the tape recorder and she typed it out, and their contemporaries continued to drift in and record their own stories. It was like a confessional and it was helping to alleviate their boredom at being stuck in the castle.

'Everybody wants to get in on the act,' she told

Callum, and switched on the tape-recorder for him, and he roared with laughter as he listened. 'What are you going to call it?' she asked. 'Sixty scandalous years?'

'In a very limited edition,' he said. 'But you're doing a grand job.'

It was by her own choice that she spent so much time in the office, but she was there from morning till night because Tom Corbishley was not the only man who had expected to be back at his own desk by now. She typed out memos and drafts, dull and detailed stuff, and getting it down on paper took some of the steam out of their frustration at this enforced holiday.

Callum gave her work to do too. She listened to his voice and typed out his words and was always slightly surprised that her fingers hit the right keys because his deep slow voice could liquefy her bones. She had, and always would have, a tremendous crush on him, but she did have it in check and she congratulated herself on how sensible she was being.

Besides, her work was appreciated. Everybody said thank you and there was to be a settling up before the businessmen left here, and Callum was fairly considerate about it. He asked several times if it was all right by her, working long office hours. 'Don't you mind?' he said, when he put more work down on her table, and it might have been a rhetorical question, because she always said, 'Not at all,' and she didn't.

She was earning and there was nothing else she wanted to do. She 'kept herself to herself', something she had never done before. She had always been an outgoing girl but now she cut off from everything outside this room. Her more or less constant companion was Hyde, and what was happening to the rest of them she learned by hearsay.

She ate her meals in the kitchens and there she was told—not by Mrs Fraser who was against gossiping— that some of the younger ones were getting restless, that there was partner-swapping and sharp words and the laundry was a never-ending problem. But the sisters stayed happy and Rosalie was radiant.

Morag never saw Rosalie. She never came across her coming downstairs in the morning, or on her way to the kitchens, or going back to her room at night. The only folk Morag talked to were the staff in the kitchens and whoever came into the office, but she knew that Rosalie was bearing up marvellously and looking fantastic.

On the fifth day it stopped snowing but the gales roared on. Islanders who had been caught in the castle on New Year's Day struggled back to their homes, most of them returning here to what was quite a pleasant and well paid job, looking after the guests. There were a few new faces, and news from the little town around the bay. Some of the guests ventured out, although it was bitterly cold and the wind leapt on them like a starving animal. But after a few of them were blown over, and Lady Ensor was carried back with a sprained ankle, they gave that up and stayed indoors.

Through the clear air now you could see the sea from the castle windows, mountainous waves and black churning water. No boat would be coming over that, Calla was still in the grip of some of the worst weather in living memory.

So it went on. The island was cut off for ten days in all. It was not a record by a long way but this was only the beginning of January and the moment the lull came everyone was frantic to escape. By the morning of the tenth day contact had been made with the mainland and all the guests were packed and waiting. A helicopter landed and there was a rush of departing businessmen. A little fleet of boats entered the harbour and a stream of cars took off from the castle.

They left disorder behind them, several weeks' work for Mrs Fraser and her domestics, and leaving the sisters in need of a rest. They also left Morag better off by a healthy sum. She had been paid for her secretarial work, some cheques, some cash, and she was not in the first rush to leave Calla. It had been more than ever like the *Titanic* in the end, all that elbowing for the lifeboats. Flora had pleaded, 'You won't be leaving us just yet will you?' the morning of the exodus, and Morag had promised to stay a little longer.

She stayed in the office, where anyone who wanted her could find her. The businessmen came to pay up and some of the guests to say goodbye but not Rosalie. And early afternoon Callum looked in to pack a briefcase, frowning over papers, as impatient to be off as any of them.

I hope you were bored she thought. I hope these ten days started to drag very soon.

As he snapped down the case catches he said, 'Thank you for all you've done, these last ten days have been equal to three months.' He smiled. 'You've earned your brother a remittance, we'll discuss it later.'

'All right,' she said.

When Callum had gone the castle seemed emptied. By that time it almost was. Kevin had left without a goodbye. Morag saw him with his case packed, standing in the hall which was looking like a departure lounge, and he stared straight through her and then turned away. He wanted no further contact with Morag, and that was fair enough.

As soon as the final goodbyes were said, Mrs Fraser started marshalling her forces for starting tomorrow on an early spring clean. Before the extra staff were paid off, dustsheets would be back and rooms would be shut up, because there were unlikely to be any more guests for a long time. None of them was going to risk getting marooned here again this winter.

It seemed strange to Morag to hear no sound but her own footsteps when she walked along a corridor and to know that all the rooms were empty again. For the first time since New Year's Eve she went up to the schoolroom. She knew that Rosalie was supposed to be sitting for her portrait but it was a little shock to see the canvas still on the easel and Rosalie smiling at her between the sisters. She looked breathless and beautiful, teeth showing like pearls between parted lips.

'Not bad,' said Morag. 'Not bad at all.' Kevin must have gone off with the payment for this, and a tale to tell them back home. Not everybody had spent the last weeks cut off from the world in a Scottish castle. What he would tell them about Morag goodness knows. Except that he hoped he never saw her again.

The odds were he never would. She had no particular plans except that she would stay a little longer on Calla but she would do her best to avoid Kevin in the future.

Next morning she sat at Callum's desk, typing and taking 'phone calls. The day was clear, although the temperature stayed well below freezing, and the sisters had decided to risk a car ride. Hamish had set off, with them swathed in furs in the back seat of the Daimler, driving very carefully. At the speed he was going Morag felt they should be safe enough.

Since the 'phones were reconnected there had been quite a number of calls. This morning's were all for the sisters and Callum, although Morag was half expecting Alistair to call her. She took down names and messages and she recognised Rosalie's voice at once, and wrote 'Rosalie——' on the message pad and said, 'I'm sorry but they're out. They insisted . . .'

'That's Morag isn't it?'

'Yes.'

'I've got something to tell you.' She didn't want to know. Whatever it was she did not want to know. 'This might be rather a shock to you but Callum and I are getting married as soon as we can get a special licence,' said Rosalie in her breathless little-girl voice and there was a roaring in Morag's ears, drowning everything.

She could not bear it. She would not listen. But she was paralysed, still holding the receiver against her cheek, and now Rosalie was saying something about a quiet wedding, no fuss, and the sisters would be disappointed wouldn't they? And then, 'I hope you'll forgive me if you did care for him, Callum promised me there was nothing between you.'

Rosalie had always suspected that Morag carried a torch for Callum. She wasn't gloating. She was the winner and she was being sympathetic and rather sweet as she pleaded, 'Please don't hate me, I don't want to hurt you. I don't want to hurt anybody, but those days and nights on Calla were so wonderful and we are so very much in love. I was just a girl before, now—I'm a woman.'

'Don't worry,' said Morag. 'There was nothing between us. Have a nice life.' She kept her hand pressed down on the 'phone. If it had rung again she could not have answered it but it didn't, and a bone-deep chill crept through her.

She had never believed this would happen. She had fooled herself that ten days of Rosalie would warn Callum against spending his life with her. She had thought that time was on her own side, and that was why she was still here now, waiting for when he would put the sable coat around her again and they would go walking in the north wing. Or when he would simply reach out a hand for her and say 'Morag,' as though her name was as deep inside him as 'Callum' was in her, beating like her heart.

Not now. Now there was nothing to wait for. She dialled the antiques centre and left the message, 'Would you tell Alistair I'll be back at the end of the week.' She packed a case and caught the ferry.

The speed and ease of her departure was fantastic. It was as though everything combined to get her off Calla without hassle, from when she went down to tell Mrs

Fraser that she had decided to leave after all. Mrs Fraser wasn't blaming anybody who had just seen winter on Calla, and realised that if they missed this chance there might not be another for a long time.

The ferry was in the harbour. Mrs Fraser said she would explain to the sisters and Morag climbed into the Range Rover with her case. Four hours later she landed at Oban.

The mainland lay under deep snow, closing airports, and she travelled by rail and road in fits and starts. She stayed in small hotels on the way; Crianlarich, Glasgow, Carlisle, Preston, Birmingham. Each night a different almost empty dining room, and a different bedroom so empty that she felt like the last living soul on earth.

She was in no hurry to get anywhere. There was a raw aching inside her like an open wound. A few days wouldn't heal it, neither would a few years, but during this long slow journey she built up an outer carapace of calm.

In bitter weather she walked each town in turn, wandered around shops, went to a cinema, a theatre, and read paperbacks late into the night.

On the sixth day she 'phoned Alistair from Birmingham and again she left a message. It was late afternoon, and the man who answered asked her to hold on while he looked around for Alistair. 'No need,' she said. 'Would you just say that Morag 'phoned and I'll be along this evening?'

'Hello Morag,' said Carl, expert in old coins and medals. 'Awful weather. Not doing much for trade.'

'Not doing much for anything,' said Morag. 'See you all tomorrow.'

'If you don't brighten the place up,' said Carl gallantly, 'nothing will.'

She didn't feel bright. She felt full with misery when the bus stopped in the town square of Moreton Meadows and she got out with her case. It was a winter's scene. Although pavements and roads had been gritted and cleared there were still piles of hard dingy snow, and the few folk around were muffled against the freezing air. But it was nothing compared to the cold and the gales of Calla.

Shops were closed but windows were alight and she walked down an almost empty street towards the centre. She was not looking forward to meeting her brother again. Since she last saw him so much had happened that was painful, she could never let him guess how painful, but she was almost sure she could tell him she had kept her part of the bargain, and from now on Callum would go easier on the repayments.

Now she was free again. If the dealers still needed casual help she would like that. If not she would look for work, but her only real plan for the future was to blot from her mind the time she had spent on Calla. There were lights on under the eaves in Alistair's apartment, and strategic lights on all floors. The centre was closed and she put down her case and pressed the bell, giving it a good long ring although it triggered another bell up in the apartment.

She made herself smile. Her expression was cheerful and she was starting to say, 'The bad penny——' when the door opened and wiped out smile and words because it was Callum, glaring at her, demanding 'Where the hell have you been?'

Funny you should say that, she thought; how right you are! 'What are you doing here?' she asked wearily and stepped inside without her case.

He stepped out and picked it up and then led the way, ahead of her through the silent centre, up the stairs. His silhouette was a dark moving shadow, his broad shoulders seemed to blot out the light and she could hardly drag herself after him. Her boots seemed heavy as lead and she was as exhausted as if she had gone nights without sleep, come to that she hadn't had restful nights lately. But she had thought she would be safe here. She had expected the odd 'phone call, the sisters would be sorry to lose her, she had thought they might try to lure her back; but not *Callum*! She had thought she was safe from him and she remembered, muzzily, reading something that somebody had said, 'If I run from him for a thousand years he will always be part of my blood.'

He would. So running was useless and there was no strength left in her. She was sick and tired and it was so cruelly unfair and what was he *doing* here, and where was Alistair?

Because as soon as she walked in she knew that the apartment was empty, and that there was only herself and Callum in all this great building. She would not sit down. Somehow she kept her backbone stiff, her head up and her voice clear and sharp. 'What's all this about? You said I'd served my time, and I suddenly felt I'd had enough of winter on Calla.'

'I'm sorry Rosalie broke the news to you,' he said. 'I'd have preferred to have done it myself.'

She gave a hoot of derision. 'Such consideration!'

'That was why you left Calla?'

She managed an elaborate shrug and asked, 'Is it true?'

'Yes.'

'Of course. All those days and nights cooped up in the castle changed her from girl to woman, was how Rosalie put it.' Knives were twisting inside her. 'So how come you're here to chat me up?'

Unbelievably he said, 'It's only your pride that's hurt. I won't believe that you are.'

'How would you know?' she spat out at him. 'You know nothing about me. Now, if you don't mind.' She marched into the little room that was her bedroom, slamming the door behind her, but he followed so close that it immediately swung open again and she rounded on him furiously. 'You're not getting me back to Calla. I suppose the Flora-Doras want me back.'

'I want you,' he said, and the arrogance of that stunned her for a moment, and she was in his arms and his mouth was on hers and she felt the kiss in every nerve, like sweet fire. She jerked her head back, baring her teeth, shaking her head from side to side, and he groaned, 'Don't fight me. I can make you happy if you'll just let me.'

And for a little while he could. The sexual attraction between them was a dynamite that could blot out everything else for her, and as suicidal as dynamite. He knew that. He thought he could have them both, Morag and Rosalie, and she screamed, 'Go away. Go away.'

'I'm going no further than outside that door,' he said. 'Just calm down and then come out and talk to me.'

She wondered if she was going out of her mind. 'Let's get this straight. You're propositioning me?'

He turned in the open doorway to look back at her. 'That's one way of putting it.'

This must be a record, even for the black Maconnells, setting himself up with a wife and a mistress all in a week. Hysterical laughter was rising in her throat, threatening to choke her. 'When is the wedding?' she croaked. 'Or have I missed it?'

'The arguments are still going on. Kevin Sanders isn't quite what Rosalie's family had in mind.' He closed the door behind him and the name exploded in her head.

Kevin ... *KEVIN?* Rosalie had said, 'Callum and I are getting married as soon as we can get a special licence,' and 'Callum promised me there was nothing between you.' Callum ... Kevin ... there was a similarity, and Morag had been so sure that Callum was the name she would hear, but it was Kevin that Rosalie had been babbling about.

Suddenly the room was filled with sunlight. How had this happened? Nobody had said Rosalie and Kevin were starting an affair. Nobody had known. So how, and when? While she was sitting for her portrait? That would have given them talking time, and Kevin was a fast worker, and if Rosalie finally realised that Callum was never going to get seriously involved with her—and she thought Kevin looked like a Greek god—during those days and nights on Calla he could have become her secret lover, her great romance.

The sisters would be devastated, but Morag was filled with a joyous wave of relief so that tears were not far away. She wanted to run into Callum's arms and cry her eyes out because this last week had been hellish, but when she opened the bedroom door and saw him standing by the window she was suddenly scared that maybe even yet there was a gulf between them.

He looked as grim as he had done when they had first faced each other in this room, before she left for Calla. Still in boots and great coat she sat, as she had done that morning, on the sofa, and said, 'Everybody was saying that you and she—she looked so lovely at the ball.'

'She did,' said Callum. 'She does. I'm fond of Rosalie and I hope she'll be happy with him, but frankly I don't care who he has so long as it isn't you. If I'd heard you were marrying him I'd have cut his throat.'

Her eyes widened. '*You* were jealous of *Kevin*?' That was so crazy that she laughed.

'Take it from me, the genuine article is no laughing matter,' he said wryly.

I know she thought, I know it well. 'New Year's Eve was not a good time for me,' he said. 'I couldn't trust myself near you that night. If I'd got my hands on you I'd never have let you go again.'

Sometime she would explain how her dress got torn, tell him she had slept alone. She asked, 'Where did you sleep that night?'

'In the room off the office. It would have been a ridiculous situation if Rosalie had come to my room and she might have done.' He walked towards the chair opposite her, sat down, watching her. 'Why?'

'I thought you slept with Rosalie. You nearly got yourself killed getting back to her next day.'

'That was nothing to do with Rosalie. I wasn't leaving you alone with Sanders if the island was getting cut off. I got back to make sure that what with the memoirs and the typing you didn't have much time to spend with him. I thought time was on my side if I could keep you apart.'

'Did you know about them?' she asked.

'Not until the day they left. I didn't think it would matter that much to you.' He was still speaking quietly. Now his voice rose slightly, sounding as if he was making a superhuman effort to control it. A weaker man would have shouted, 'I still will not accept that it does,' but Callum was on his feet again, walking away from her, standing at the window with his back to her.

'I came back to Calla the day you left, and I've been waiting for you ever since. Wherever you go I'll be, because I lied when I said you could never get near me. You are in me, part of me. We two have belonged together since God-knows-when. I knew it in here that first day. When I heard that 'phone call from your brother I tried to leave you but I couldn't, I can't. So don't tell me to get away because there is no place either of us can go to get away from the other.'

Morag whispered, 'I thought she said Callum.'

'What?' He turned.

'I thought Rosalie said Callum on the 'phone, not Kevin. It wasn't too good a line, I wasn't hearing too well. I thought she was marrying you.'

For the first time she saw him at a loss for words. He stared in amazement. 'You believed that?'

'Until then,' she said, 'I thought time was on *my* side. I hoped Rosalie would bore you.'

'Rosalie does.' She stood up as he came towards her.

'*Morag* . . .' He said her name as she had dreamed of him saying it, and he put out his arms and pulled her against him, and they clung together as if nothing could part them again in this life nor the next.

'Where the hell *have* you been?' he said. 'I've been in touch with every friend you ever had.'

'Small hotels. I had folding money, thanks to your business friends. Where's Alistair? You haven't shoved him in a cupboard?'

'He'll be back with the rest of them tomorrow.'

'That's accommodating of him.' Not that he would have any choice. 'How did the sisters take the news about Rosalie and Kevin?' And Callum grinned.

'Not so well. But they cheered up when I told them I had long-term plans for you.'

She could smell his aftershave faintly, his hard brown jawline was smooth. He must have shaved while he waited for her and she couldn't breathe in enough of him. She breathed now deeply and said, 'What did you tell them?'

'That you are the only woman I want for a wife, that you're the one I'm planning to marry.'

She loved him so much that when she looked at him, wordlessly, he must surely know her answer.

He said, 'The short-term plan I didn't tell them.'

'Tell me.'

'To make love to you as soon as I could get you alone. Using fair means or foul, any way I could, to make you forget Kevin Sanders and never want loving from anyone but me again.'

She was still bundled in thick clothing, beneath all the layers her skin was glowing but she shivered in anticipation of his touch. 'Put your brand on me?' she said.

'Why not? I carry yours.'

'Not easy,' she said, 'through this lot.' She moved towards the open door and the shadowy bedroom, her hand in his, her face alight with love and laughter. 'Come inside love,' she said.

Here's how to get this special offer from Harlequin!
As simple as 1...2...3!

BONUS
TREASURY EDITION
COUPON

1. Each month, save one Treasury Edition coupon from your favorite Romance or Presents novel.
2. In four months you'll have saved four Treasury Edition coupons (only one coupon per month allowed).
3. Then all you have to do is fill out and return the order form provided, along with the four Treasury Edition coupons required and $1.00 for postage and handling.

Mail to: Harlequin Reader Service

In the U.S.A.
2504 West Southern Ave.
Tempe, AZ 85282

In Canada
P.O. Box 2800, Postal Station A
5170 Yonge Street
Willowdale, Ont. M2N 6J3

Please send me my FREE copy of the Janet Dailey Treasury Edition. I have enclosed the four Treasury Edition coupons required and $1.00 for postage and handling along with this order form.

(Please Print)

NAME_____

ADDRESS_____

CITY_____

STATE/PROV._____ ZIP/POSTAL CODE_____

SIGNATURE_____

This offer is limited to one order per household.

SUPPLIES LIMITED

This special Janet Dailey offer expires January 1986.

Take 4 novels and a surprise gift FREE